TWILIGHT CHRISTMAS

A Carolina Coast Novella

Normandie Fischer

Sleepy Creek Press

Sleepy Creek Press
PO Box 114
Gloucester, NC, 28528
www.sleepycreekpress.com

Publisher's Note: This is a work of fiction. Names, characters, places, and incidents are a product of the author's imagination. Locales and public names are sometimes used for atmospheric purposes. Any resemblance to actual people, living or dead, or to businesses, companies, events, institutions, or locales is completely coincidental.

Book Layout ©2013 BookDesignTemplates.com
Cover Design, Normandie Fischer with thanks to photographers from Unsplash.com

Ordering Information:
Quantity sales. Special discounts are available on quantity purchases by corporations, associations, and others. For details, contact the "Special Sales Department" at the address above.

Twilight Christmas/Normandie Fischer -- 1st ed.
ISBN 978-0-9861416-9-0

Dedicated to Finn Alexander Scoville
Blessings of kindness and strength to you, my
beloved grandson. May you always live up to your
name as a fair defender of men.

Perfect love casts out fear.

–JOHN 4:18

O Twilight! Spirit that dost render birth
To dim enchantments—melting heaven to earth—
Leaving on craggy hills and running streams
A softness like the atmosphere of dreams.

–MRS. NORTON

Hail, twilight! sovereign of one peaceful hour!

–WORDSWORTH

How beautiful the silent hour, when morning and
evening thus sit together, hand in hand, beneath the
starless sky of midnight!

–LONGFELLOW

1 LOUIS

Louis drew his hand back from his mama's cheek. No matter how many times he shook her, cried out to her, begged her, she stayed cold and gray. No breath, no tears, no nothing.

He wanted the images of her blank eyes and her pale lips undone. Once upon a time, those lips had smiled around her snaggletooth, one just like his, but it would never catch or embarrass her again.

He wanted last night back. Last night she'd still been alive. Last night she hadn't smelled funny.

He took a step away from her bed. He'd leave the empty pill bottle at her side and not even try to close her eyes like he'd seen them do on TV. The police would figure out how she'd died, what she'd taken, what had finally let her out of this life and her need to be a mother to them.

He bit hard on his lower lip. He would not get angry at how she'd left them, left him, to cope.

He didn't hear Linney pad in and couldn't stop her before she climbed up beside the mama who wasn't there. As she reached a hand toward Mama's cheek, he cried out. "No! Don't touch."

But she already had. A quick touch. A quick moan. A barely heard "Cold." And then, "Ma . . . ma? Wake up," said with the beginning of tears.

He called Linney to him, but she just sat there uncomprehending. He swiped at his nose. It kept leaking, like his eyes did, and his tears fogged up his glasses. He pulled them off, wiped them on his shirt, wiped his eyes with his hands, then stuck his too-loose frames back on his nose and tried to get control of himself. He had to stop acting like a baby so he could fix things. Soon as they found out his mama was dead, they'd come take him and Linney, and they'd put Linney one place and him another.

Just like last time.

"Come on. I'll . . . I'll fix your breakfast." He reached for his sister's hand. He could do this. He had to do this.

Linney looked once more at the body that wasn't their mama anymore and trailed behind him to the kitchen area.

"Sit," he said before he turned back to close the bedroom door, softly, as if anything else might wake the sleeping.

If only it would. If only it would.

He couldn't think about that. Instead, he got out the sugared cereal Linney shouldn't eat in spite of it being her favorite, filled a bowl with the last of it, poured in milk, and set it before her. She smiled brilliantly up at him.

He couldn't eat a single thing. Not until he figured out what to do and how to fix this.

Mama kept her old suitcase stuffed with summer clothes 'cause the trailer didn't have enough room for more drawers. He dragged it from behind the couch, opened it, and took out everything they didn't need. Then he went to Linney's room and got some warm things for her, then some for him. He stuffed those in and remembered he'd need plenty of pull-up diapers for his sister. And the wipe things, in case she had an accident. If she was scared or upset, accidents happened. Too many times. And he hated having to help her, now she was getting older.

It shouldn't be him. It really shouldn't.

But who else was there? Who else had there been most nights?

To make the pull-ups fit in the suitcase he had to take out some of his clothes, including his extra sweater. Linney needed more changes of clothes anyway. He could make do. He tried to decide which of his books he should bring. No way he wanted to get stupid just 'cause he couldn't go to school anymore.

Then he checked around to see if he'd forgotten anything.

The cops would come hunting them if he left the trailer looking like this. While Linney watched, he put everything in order, the way Mama would have, before he sat down to write a note in his best cursive, copying Mama's writing, fixing things so no one would come looking.

He'd wait until dark. Then he'd fill a sack with other things he'd need and figure out how to get him and Linney and their stuff to a good hiding place. He had time to figure it out.

Figuring out how to make Linney understand why Mama wasn't in the body back there was gonna be harder. She'd never understand death, but she was a good girl. A four-year-old trapped in the body of a twelve-year-old but with none of the attitude he'd seen on other kids. Linney was the smilingest, happiest girl he knew.

And she was his responsibility.

He took out another piece of paper and tried to make a list of the hows and the wheres. He had to do this right if he was gonna fix things. Find a place, find a way, and use the time until dark to plan their future. He'd already emptied Mama's hiding jar and counted out the bills. It was enough for now, but then what? Money and running out of it was his biggest fear.

Next to being found and having someone bad get Linney, like had happened to that other girl in special ed.

2 ANNIE MAC

The ancient furnace chugged on. Minutes later it shuddered, whined, and quit. Annie Mac registered the noises, but barely, and then she slid deeper into sleep.

And back into the dream.

She wasn't certain whether the cold or the dream woke her. She knew she'd cried out, and she was sitting up in the bed.

What a mess.

Both she and the furnace were disasters waiting to happen.

She checked the bright red numbers on the clock. Three forty-three. Perhaps if she picked up a soothing book, she'd find a temporary place where sleep could slide in peacefully.

Perhaps. But first she should check on the children.

A storm raged off the coast and had been met by a low pressure system swooping down from Canada, causing temperatures to plummet in Beaufort, North Carolina. This was not the night to be without heat, not in a house with single-paned windows and uninsulated walls.

Ty always flung off covers. When she pulled them up again and added a quilt to the mass, he behaved like a typical almost-teen and didn't stir. Five-year-old Katie did, squirming to resettle and plugging her thumb between her lips.

Annie Mac drew heavy socks over toes that wouldn't warm on their own and snuggled under her quilt with a Charles Martin book she'd been reading. Getting lost in the pages of one of Martin's books usually changed her mood, but his stories of strong and valiant heroes brought comparisons into sharp relief, the fictional and the real. If only she'd read his stories when she'd been young. If only she'd known there were options, that not all strong men behaved like her harsh and judgmental father, that pretty and easy-going didn't equate with kind and loving. Maybe she wouldn't have made one mistake on top of the other. Maybe then she'd have been able to accept the love of the one good man who'd ever shown up in her life.

Her internal clock woke her much too early for a cold December morning. The idea of leaving her warm cocoon for frigid rooms had her snuggling under the covers and shutting her eyes.

Eventually, though, even the pretense of sleep failed, and she rose to begin her day. Ty and Katie would linger in bed, taking advantage of two days off because of optional teacher workdays. The optional part meant she could work from home and be here for them.

She dressed hurriedly in jeans, a turtleneck, and a heavy sweater, and headed to the kitchen, wishing it were late enough to call about the furnace. While her kettle heated and while her tea steeped, she made notes of all she had to accomplish—including the non-optional task of tallying her students' grades and preparing progress reports before Christmas break.

Her hot mug warmed her hands, and the quilt she'd dragged with her warmed her back and shoulders, but if someone didn't come fix that furnace soon, she might actually utter a few words better left unspoken.

By the time she finished her list and her tea, it was after eight, surely not too early to call the property manager. He didn't have the day off, which meant someone ought to pick up.

No one did.

Fine. Whatever. She left a message. And, yes, she was nice about it.

And then she retrieved her school folder and got to work before her children woke. Her afternoon would be busy. Katie had an appointment for a check-up, and

Ty was supposed to spend the afternoon at his friend Jilly's.

He'd like that. And tonight he'd get to stay over at Clay's so they could have another sailing lesson in the morning. He needed to pack his bag for that.

And make promises to his mother that he wouldn't drown.

In spite of wanting to keep her boy to herself, she knew he needed a male role model. She just hated that he'd picked Detective Lieutenant Clay Dougherty, the man who'd saved their life and given them a home when they'd needed one. Oh, and by the way, the man she was probably in love with. If she knew anything about love.

And if love existed for someone like her. How could it exist for a woman who cringed from a good man because the last man had used his fists, had used force, and still showed up in her nightmares?

No, Ty would have to settle for these occasional days and overnights with his idol. Hah. This was almost like a divorce with visitation rights for the kids.

But it had to be this way. It did.

It took the realtor three hours to return her call, but she eventually extracted a promise that someone would tend to the furnace. Perhaps this time the fix would be longer lasting.

"Time to go!" she called toward the bedrooms.

It amazed her how quickly kids could be herded into a car when they were off to play instead of heading to school. And going to Jilly's was particularly fun. Normally, they'd walk the short distance between houses, but Katie's appointment was clear across the bridge into Morehead.

Jilly waved when Annie Mac pulled up next to the Merritt's back yard. "Brisa's here, too! Come on, let's play!"

"Me, too!" Katie tried to free herself before her mother could even open the door.

"Hang on," Annie Mac said and helped her down. "We're only going to be here a few minutes."

"Okay!"

Tadie, Jilly's step-mother, greeted them from the porch. Holding her very wiggly one-year-old son, she introduced Annie Mac to their new neighbors, Agnes and her daughter, Brisa, who'd just moved to Beaufort from New Jersey. Brisa was a knockout with her caramel-colored skin and thick black hair, and her mama seemed nice.

Blond, red, and black heads all racing around the yard together made Annie Mac want to grab a camera to capture the wonder of childhood joy. Which just sent her heart into a flutter that was half thrill and half pain. Her babies. Laughing, running, unafraid, the terror of last year maybe not forgotten but certainly set aside and fading into a past that no longer held them captive.

If only she could let it go as easily.

She chatted with the other two women, not really registering much as she thought of all she had to accomplish today. And then she excused herself. "We'd better get going."

Katie pouted and protested that she didn't want to leave the fun. Of course she didn't.

"We'll see how much time we have when we pick up your brother," Annie Mac said, before she remembered Ty would have to get ready to spend the night away from home. The constriction returned, and she sighed. "At any rate, you and I will have fun. We'll do some shopping after our appointment and then get an ice cream. How does that sound?"

"'Nilla?" Katie asked around her thumb.

"Perfect."

Tadie walked with them to the car, Sammy still attached to her hip, and stood to one side as Annie Mac buckled Katie into her booster seat. "I didn't want to say anything in front of Brisa and her mama, because I don't think they're into church activities, but I assume your two will be in the pageant this year?"

"They will. I'll be working on costumes."

"I was wondering if you'd mind taking Jilly with you when you go. She's looking forward to being part of it again, and—"

"And you have Sammy. We'd love for Jilly to go with us. After all you've done for me and mine?"

"Don't be silly. We're friends. Anyway, you want to bring Katie by after her appointment, she'll be welcome."

"Appreciate it, but she'll need a nap after we finish at the store."

"You probably will, too."

Annie Mac grinned. "You know it. I only have patience to deal with my fourth graders if I'm not exhausted."

"You sleeping okay these days?"

"Most nights. Thank you for asking." She slid in behind the wheel and buckled her seatbelt. "I'll call you when I get back. Clay invited Ty to spend the night. They're sailing tomorrow, if the weather cooperates."

Tadie glanced over her shoulder at the back yard where Ty chased the two girls. "Why don't you tell Clay to pick up Ty here? You could bring his overnight things later."

"That's tempting." It would mean she wouldn't have to see Clay until he brought Ty back tomorrow. She wouldn't have to yearn—or see the yearning reflected in Clay's expression. "Thanks, Tadie."

She backed out onto Front Street and headed away from town. First things first. The doctor, the store, and then the rest of the day—with her baby, her sweetest little girl, who would never have to be afraid again. Not if Annie Mac had anything to say about it.

She remembered the anniversary while bagging her groceries. There was nothing remarkable about the plastic sack in her hands, and nothing about the process that should have focused her thoughts and brought back the memory. But remember she did.

It had been four years since Auntie Sim's death. Four years since that precious woman had left her alone in a house that would see too much violence and too much pain.

"Oh, Auntie Sim, I miss you." She glanced at the small floral section near the produce. From where she stood, nothing looked fresh enough to last the night. They'd stop at the farmer's market on the way to the cemetery and buy some bulbs that would bloom in the spring. That would have to be after she filled the car with gas and put the cold items away and took Ty's duffel to Tadie's.

Katie would just have to go with her and nap in the car. Because Annie Mac was not going to miss honoring the woman who'd rescued her and given her a life when her parents had shown her teenaged self the highway.

She leaned toward Katie. "What do you think, sweetie? You want to take flowers to Auntie Sim? And plant some for spring?"

The thumb broke suction but remained between her lips. "I love fwowers."

"I know you do. Will you help me pick out some pretty ones?"

"Yeth, ma'am." The thumb came out. "When can I have ice cream?"

"We'll get some at the plant nursery. They've got a nice market there." And she hoped they still sold cones in winter.

At least last night's storm had passed, and with every hour of daylight, the warmth had spread. It was now a balmy sixty-five, according to the flashing sign at the bank. Sixty-five would be perfect for planting bulbs.

Storms passed. They always did.

Ice cream drips dotted Katie's light jacket and ran down her fingers and chin. Annie Mac grabbed a baby wipe and scrubbed off what she could and then collected the pot of crocuses, the new trowel, and several bottles of water. Katie held out her hands to help.

"Here you go." Annie Mac handed her a water bottle and led the way to the plot where a simple stone marked her auntie's grave.

Katie marched beside her, waving the bottle like a baton and extending it when they arrived. "Here, Mommy, you take it," she said. "I'm gonna go see the angels."

"Don't wander. Stay where you can see me, and where I can see you."

Katie skipped up to the stone guardians that watched over a largish family plot, and Annie Mac knelt to dig a hole. Auntie Sim would have loved the crocuses, so like ones she'd grown and tended in her yard. The loss of Sim hurt like a knife poking at her gut—a very pointy knife.

"I miss you so much." She dashed a wayward tear with fingers that had probably smeared dirt across her cheek. "I hope you know. I hope you saw what happened to Roy, because we're doing just fine. Except, I could use some of your wisdom." The whisper of a breeze picked up a strand of her hair, glossed its way over her face. "I could sure use one of your hugs."

As if she'd heard her mommy's words, Katie skipped over and leaned against Annie Mac's bowed back. "Angels, Mama."

Annie Mac dropped the bulbs into the ground and turned to draw her baby close. "I see them."

"I'm gonna be one for Christmas."

"Won't that be fun?"

"You ready t'go?"

"Almost. I just have a couple more things to finish."

"'kay!" Katie danced back to the statues.

As Annie Mac covered the area around the bulbs with additional dirt, something caught her eye, a flash of black. A crow sauntered across the empty plot beside her.

She fell back on her heels. That was the plot meant for her. And a crow walked on it, cawing as if she were the intruder.

What had Auntie Sim said? "It's a comfort to me, little girl. You not having to worry about this. And someday—not too soon, mind you—you'll be lying there, next to me. You're my family."

Annie Mac swiped at more tears even as the scent of turned earth engulfed her. The empty spot seemed to leer. *You were this close*, it whispered, *this close to decaying here, years ahead of time.* He'd almost killed her. Roy. Killed her and taken Katie.

Shaken, she brushed herself off, gathered her things, and hurried toward the car with her precious one, trying not to cling too tightly, trying not to hear that crow's caw as a presage of disaster. On the drive home, she tried to play the mind games her counselor had suggested, that litany of safety, while keeping a smile pasted on for her little girl's sake.

It had only been a crow.

3 ANNIE MAC

After a dinner of macaroni and cheese, Annie Mac read two chapters from *Winnie-the-Pooh* with her sweet girl curled in her lap. Then it was bath time, followed by another chapter once Katie'd climbed in bed, and, finally, goodnight prayers.

"Sleep well, my princess." Annie Mac pulled the extra quilt over her little one, because the furnace was still out.

Of course it was still out. Why should anyone else care if their noses froze?

Okay, fine, the temperature probably wouldn't drop below fifty overnight. But that shouldn't matter. She paid rent for what was supposed to be a heated apartment.

"Mama, I do get to be an angel in the play, don't I? For real?"

"You do. And Ty will be a shepherd."

"An angel's important, isn't she?"

"Yes, ma'am." Annie Mac nuzzled her daughter's nose. "She gets to announce that baby Jesus has been born."

"Do I get wings?"

"You do."

"And a halo?"

"A lovely silver halo." She kissed the sweet cheek. "Good night, my love. Sleep tight."

She left nightlights burning in Katie's room and in the hall and wandered through the chilly apartment before deciding to seek comfort by snuggling in her own bed. The story she picked up should have been compelling enough to keep her awake, but here she was, yawning, her eyelids heavy.

After one last trip to the bathroom, she turned off her light and closed her eyes. Nothing. She stared into the dark, hoping her lids would shut on their own. They didn't.

Instead of quieting, her thoughts swirled, focusing on her small community of friends, what each was doing, what might be bothering them. Which sent her straight to worries about her own plaguy issues like lack of money and fears for her children's future.

She might as well add loneliness and world hunger to the mix.

That got her flipping to her other side, tucking and straightening her nightgown to get a wrinkle from between her thigh and the sheet. She wouldn't fix the world by staying awake. And if she didn't sleep, she wouldn't be any good to anyone.

Fine. She'd lie there with her eyes closed and pretend to sleep until it happened.

And suddenly, Roy was in the room with her.

She flailed an arm to protect her face from his curled fist. His boot connected, bones crunched, and breath hissed. The odor of rancid flesh filled her nostrils.

Scuttling backward, she screamed.

O Lord, help! God, please no . . .

And she woke.

Clutching the sheet to her breasts, she uncurled and inched down off the headboard. She lay alone in her dark room, sweating, shaking, and nauseated, but at least Roy was no more. She pressed a palm against her lips to stifle a second cry, this one from frustration and a different fear. Awake, she no longer feared a ghost. No, now she questioned her sanity.

She longed to be normal. She *tried* to be normal. But, obviously, normal wasn't happening. Not when she couldn't stop the nightmares.

She shouldn't have gone to bed so early. It was only eleven-thirty now, and she was wide awake. She tossed back her covers and pulled on her bathrobe and then tiptoed across the hall to check on her children.

The sight of Ty's empty bed startled her before she remembered. He was at Clay's. Thank God he hadn't been here to hear another scream from her.

The nightlight in Katie's room illuminated her little one's sweet face and the thumb that lay unworked in her open mouth. Annie Mac stood over the bed and listened to the breaths whispering past her daughter's lips.

How had Katie escaped unscathed?

Not for the first time, she imagined a child's guardian angel. How else could she explain Katie's unwavering trust in spite of the damage Roy had done to her as well to her mama?

Unless—and this was one of the big fears—her daughter's issues just hadn't manifested themselves yet.

She leaned over to drop a light kiss on her baby's downy cheek before wandering to the kitchen to make a cup of herbal tea. The tea company called it sleep-inducing. They lied. Or perhaps it was only soporific for those whose hearts weren't cluttered with debris.

While she waited for the water to boil, she looked for some boring reading and came across *The Life of the Blue Crab*. Ty had insisted they buy it, "Please Mama," because he needed to know all about crabs so he could catch them off Clay's dock. She smoothed her fingers over the shiny picture. Pokey eyes stared up at her, accusingly.

"Sorry," she whispered and then caught herself. She hadn't trapped and killed the fool thing.

Talking to a book cover. She was obviously on a slippery slope, and it was all downhill.

Her boy really loved Clay and had been praying for a wedding. She'd hoped for it herself, but it hadn't taken her long to figure out marriage was not for the likes of her, not after all the mistakes she'd made and the haunting she experienced when she let down her guard. She didn't deserve a man like Clay, couldn't deserve him. Tonight merely emphasized how right she'd been. Imagine if he'd slept in the bed next to her? She shuddered just thinking of it.

This was the second nightmare in a row. Sure, sometimes, like tonight, a trigger set her off, but nightmares could just as easily sneak in after a peaceful day. With that sort of record, she'd have to gut it out, because she couldn't hand over her level of craziness to another person.

She was pretty sure tonight's trigger had been her visit to the cemetery. But inciting event or no, she hated that Roy maintained any control over her. A dead man should be just that: dead.

She poured boiling water over the tea bag, stirred in a spoonful of honey, and drank it slowly, letting it warm her. It didn't make her sleepy.

Maybe the cold air would. She tightened her robe and stepped out to the small landing at the top of the stairs leading from her apartment to the ground. No one lived in the lower half of the duplex, and she was grateful for the privacy.

She stared down on a Front Street full of shadows created by the street lamps. The moon was hidden behind clouds tonight. If it were out, she'd be able to see a narrow marsh on the other side of the road, and just beyond it, Taylor's Creek. The air was redolent of salt air and plough mud, stirred up perhaps by last night's storm. In the quiet of midnight in December, she could even hear the faint lapping of water. She pulled up the collar of her bathrobe and breathed deeply.

She'd been working on her fears, the fear of drowning, fear of her babies drowning, fear of Roy coming back from the dead. Fear of making another mistake because she was so good at them.

She'd agreed to rent a place this close to the water because it was the only one she'd been able to find that had a long flight of noisy stairs. The racket they made when anyone stepped on them meant no one could sneak up without sounding an alarm. She'd hear it, hear rattles and squeaks and the scream of the motion sensor she set for nights, and she'd call for help faster than he could walk to the steel door she'd insisted on, faster than he could get all locks undone. Never again would a man smash her or her kids or her stuff with his fists. Not on her watch. And he—whoever—would have to get past her to grab either of her darlings. She'd be ready next time. All the way ready.

No way on God's green earth would she have gone back to live in the house where it had begun, that disaster from which she still recoiled. The disaster she'd let in. No, she had a tenant there, one who paid good money—or at least good enough—and she had her substitute teacher's pay. And just maybe she'd have a full-time teaching job by the first of the year.

Yes, she and her babies were safe, although she knew too well the bad things that could happen if you turned your back.

What if Clay turned his back on Ty out there on the water? Hadn't she just read about drowning victims, how they didn't *look* like they were going under for the last time, because they couldn't really flail? They just sank. And died.

She grabbed the railing, slammed shut her eyes, and forced herself to hang on. Sweat and the shakes made her throat feel as if it would close up and cut off air to her lungs. Why had she let Ty out of her sight even for one night?

Popping open her lids so she wouldn't fall, she backed toward the wall, gulping air even as she worked to turn her mind to truths. Ty could swim, and he always wore a life vest. Clay had promised.

Breathe. Release. Breathe. Release.

Ty can *swim.*

She'd finally steeled herself to let Ty and Katie take swimming lessons. She remembered the chlorine scent of the water, the moldy odor in the pool showers. She'd known those as a child. Known the fear. Remembered her father forcing her in, forcing her to swim, almost forcing her to drown. And thinking her worthless because she couldn't stop sobbing or shivering or begging.

Footsteps sounded on the sidewalk below, even as late as this, and a light laugh slid across the night air, as if somebody were mighty pleased with life. Annie Mac peered down at the retreating figure silhouetted in the lamplight before she went back inside, closed and locked the door.

Maybe now she'd be able to sleep. It had looked like Agnes down there, heading home from her job at Aqua. Annie Mac would think about what Agnes and her daughter must have to deal with, not about herself. Or her babies.

Or the nightmares that wouldn't leave her be.

She rubbed her hands across her stomach. Then she whispered the litany: "Ty is fine. Katie's fine. *I* am fine. Ty is fine, Katie's fine, *I* am fine."

She didn't want to be the crazy mother who raised crazy kids. There had to be an answer, somewhere. Because, if there weren't, she didn't know how she'd cope. The thing about being crazy, the real truth that scared the daylights out of her, was that sooner or later folk would find out, and when they did, she'd lose her job, and then she'd lose her babies, and then she'd die.

4 CLAY

Clay Dougherty padded barefoot into his kitchen and set the kettle on to boil before getting out his French press and grinding enough beans for a good strong cup of Sumatra. While he waited for the water to come just shy of a boil, he opened the blinds shielding the great room from the early morning sunlight bouncing off the creek.

Perfect. The sun was doing its job of warming the air and the water, making it ideal weather for a day of sailing. He glanced toward the guest hall where the boy lay asleep in his old room.

And something cracked open a little wider in Clay.

He rubbed away the image of the second bedroom, empty of the woman who'd occupied it not that long ago. The what-ifs, the could-bes did him no good at all.

No, it was a gorgeous, unseasonably warm day, and he was away from work, away from the demands of the station house, which admittedly had been limited to petty crimes this week. And last week.

Luckily, the murder they'd solved in early November justified their pay. A husband had left his wife for his mistress. Only, the suspect—the wife— hadn't plunged the knife in the guy's throat. That had been a former mistress who hadn't liked losing her sugar daddy to bimbo number two. Or number three or four, for all Clay knew. At least the wife got something out of his death, while the mistresses didn't. Except prison time for one of them. And maybe a lesson learned for the other.

More thoughts he needed to shrug off. He didn't want work issues or memories of ugliness to mar this time with Ty. Nope. That boy was one of his real joys. And teaching him to sail? A huge perk. Huge.

He poured hot water over the coffee grounds and waited for the brew to steep. Then he got out a mixing bowl, flour, eggs, and milk, and prepared to make pancakes, their favorite.

When Ty's door opened, Clay announced breakfast in five. That would get a twelve-year-old front and center.

He grinned and turned on the griddle.

Ty held up the wetsuit Clay'd bought him and then put it back in its box. "It's supposed to be seventy-five degrees this afternoon. My sweatshirt's good enough."

"One wave," Clay said, zipping up his own windbreaker, "and you'll be wet, Indian summer notwithstanding. And the water's cold. Let's at least go with this water-resistant jacket, just in case."

Ty accepted the jacket and slipped it on. Then he picked up the small cooler filled with water bottles and sandwiches and followed Clay toward the dock. Clay'd already rigged and tied up the small boat so they wouldn't have to go wading as they launched it. Wading was best left for summer.

Ty settled himself at the stern to man the tiller. Clay pushed off from the dock and sat slightly forward.

As they sailed out of the creek and into the wider waters of Core Sound, Clay said, "You need to check your mark, check the wind, and think about how high you need to point us to compensate for some leeward movement. Give yourself enough wiggle room."

Ty'd been with him a couple of times when the wind had fallen to nothing and they'd had to paddle home with the daggerboard. A lot of work, but Clay'd just flexed his biceps. "Muscles, son. Muscles." No man minded a little work, he'd said, or the results of that work.

He also remembered Ty's wide eyes the first time they'd rushed home from Cape Lookout with storm clouds looming and a hefty wind blowing up behind them. The little boat had acted like a surfboard, waves breaking over the stern and washing on past them. Ty's mama had been white-knuckled when they pulled the little boat up on shore. Annie Mac had hustled Ty into her car and lit off so fast she'd churned gravel. It had taken a whole lot of sweet talking after that to get her to let go of the boy long enough for any lessons. Didn't matter to her that Ty was safe—or that, if they'd overturned and been unable to right the boat any place out there, they'd eventually drift to one shore or another, or at least to a sand bar where they could stand. Ty had been wearing a life vest, for heaven's sake.

Annie Mac was a piece of work all right. Some of it understandable, some not. Clay still didn't know what made the woman so freakish about water. He figured she'd tell him when she was ready.

Or maybe not. He'd been so certain she was the one, so certain she thought so, too. When she said she needed time on her own to grow stronger emotionally while physical therapy helped strengthen her physically, he'd agreed. Absolutely. He'd seen the strength in her that she hadn't believed in and figured a little time to discover it couldn't hurt her or them.

What a joke. Instead, her "growth" time—the word made him gag—had hammered a wedge in deep enough to snap their obviously imaginary relationship like a dried-up log being split for kindling.

"How far we going?" Ty bent forward, checking under the boom to see what was to leeward.

Wake up, Clay told himself. "Over past marker number ten. That work for you?"

"That's on the line heading toward the Cape?"

"Yes, sir."

They weren't likely to find too many surprises out here, but you never knew. There were always stakes marking leased fishing grounds, sometimes a fishing boat anchored off a shoal. Rarely did they glimpse another sailboat.

The sun danced off the small wind waves. Ty mimicked Clay's movements when he checked the sail trim.

"Looking good," Clay told him.

As they settled into a quiet glide over the water, Ty said, "Can I talk to you about something?"

"Sure. What's on your mind?"

"Well, there's this new girl, Brisa."

Clay kept his eyes on the water to give the boy a chance to say what he wanted.

"She and her mom moved in down the street."

"Ah." Hard to tell whether Ty thought this a good thing or a bad thing.

"She likes to hang out with Jilly," Ty said.

"And Jilly's your friend."

"Yeah."

So, not something positive in Ty's mind. Ty and Jilly had bonded in the days Ty and his family'd lived out here during the mess of last year.

"Jilly never cared about girl things before." Ty leaned down to peer under the boom, keeping alert. "I mean, she was just like one of the guys. And now she wants to go off with this Brisa whenever Brisa shows up."

Clay wished he knew the right thing to say. "Doesn't Jilly want to hang out with you anymore?"

"Sure, but when Brisa comes, she wants to do girl things, even if Jilly and me are already doing other stuff. Seems to me Brisa wants Jilly for herself."

"Makes it hard." He wouldn't correct the boy's grammar. Annie Mac did that, and today wasn't for English lessons.

"Yeah."

Ty let a little of the main sheet slide between his fingers when a gust filled the sail.

"Don't you have guy friends you like to hang out with? Do things you don't do with Jilly?"

"Mostly just Andy."

"Maybe Jilly likes having a girl around who's close to her age. It doesn't mean she likes you any less. The same way you don't like Jilly less just because you also like Andy."

"I guess." Ty checked his bearings again. "Coming up on mark one."

"Can you find your second marker? You want to think about it as you round the first one."

"I see it."

"Take us there, skipper. You're doing a great job."

The joy on the boy's face every time Clay gave him a compliment made Clay's heart swell almost to bursting. It wasn't right, Annie Mac keeping them apart. The boy needed him.

And, yeah, he needed the boy.

Ty soaked up that day's lessons along with bottles of water and tuna sandwiches. When they got back to the dock several hours later, Clay touched his cap. "Skipper," he said, "that was some fine seamanship."

"Can we do it again? Maybe next time I have off school? Like Saturday?"

"Well, that's going to depend on the weather. We're nearing full-on winter, which doesn't give us many balmy sailing days. As a matter of fact, I normally put this little boat in the barn, remember? But we could find something else to do, if you're game."

A stab of anger hit Clay. Again. If only Annie Mac weren't so stubborn, he and the boy could do this and other things all the time, after school and after work. This way, he got to be a part-time uncle and always just outside their family. On the perimeter of their life.

He'd been so *sure* she loved him. So sure she'd have him.

He'd been a fool.

5 LOUIS

He'd been in a hurry the night they'd left the trailer, because no telling when one of the neighbors would come half-tumbling out his own sorry excuse for a home and see them. Yell at them. Make him say why he was hauling his sister off that time of night.

But he'd gotten them away to this old storage barn that belonged to that church across the field. While he'd been thinking where to go, trying to fix things to hide him and Linney, he'd remembered exploring the woods behind the barn and finding that loose board at the back just wide enough to let them sneak inside. He could barely see the trailer park from here, and he was pretty sure no one would think to look in a place belonging to a church that was stuffed full of junk and rusted farm equipment. Besides, the front doors to the barn had a big padlock, and a light came on if anyone got near, but he could come and go out the back with nobody seeing, as long as he didn't go when people were at the church or when those construction workers were in the lot on the barn's other side.

He'd been able to clear enough junk out of the way to make room for a kind of fort. He put some of his and Linney's stuff on top of stacked pallets and hid things he didn't want found, like the money from Mama's jar, behind the pallets or under a couple of bricks. Some light came through cracks in boards, giving him a view out the back and to the church side.

A freeze must have killed off the tangles of weeds in the woods, leaving nothing but a pile of pine needles and dying or dead stuff. He gathered a bunch of it for a bed and covered it with an opened-up garbage bag— like Mama used to use on Linney's bed—before putting one of the blankets he'd brought on top of the plastic.

Linney kept her stuffed lion close, even though it had lost one eye and half its mane was a mess. She sniffed it a lot, like a dog checking out a scent. It probably had something of Mama still on it, on account of Mama hugging both Linney and her lion at the same time. Back when she still hugged all the time.

Only, the lion wasn't Linney's baby doll. She missed that baby so much that she asked for it and woke up hunting for it. She used to carry it all the time and try to feed it, to put it to sleep. She called it Baby.

Sometimes Linney whimpered for Mama and sometimes for Baby, but Louis couldn't give her either one—Mama 'cause the dead don't live again, and Baby 'cause the doll must have fallen out of Linney's arms when he was trying to get all their stuff, along with Linney and her full arms, down the rutted cinderblock steps of the trailer and away from that life.

They mostly hid inside during the day, except sometimes when the construction workers all went to lunch and he didn't see anybody moving near the church office. He'd discovered the workmen had a portable bathroom on a trailer, and they didn't lock it. It stank, but it had a potty and a sink with a hose hooked up to it that trailed out its back and toward some kind of pipe sticking up out of the ground. The water was kinda cold, but at least it was water. When the men went off for lunch, he sometimes used it, but he waited until night to take Linney and get her cleaned up.

When they had to stay tucked away inside the barn, he read his social studies book in what light he could find, and Linney talked to her lion or played with some of the sticks and twigs he'd found so she could pretend they were blocks for building. She liked him to tell her stories, and he tried to remember some from his old books. When she got tired of those, he made up new ones.

He sometimes watched out the cracks and brought Linney over to show her squirrels racing at the woods' edge, stopping to scratch at the bed of needles to hunt for nuts or maybe berries. One night, he even heard an owl. A few birds, mostly black or brown ones, showed up and made him long to be free to roam. Free to go.

Each time he thought of taking off, he just had to look over at Linney to know he couldn't. He wouldn't.

He'd brought enough food with them for a few days, cans of soup, bread, a package of hot dogs, but it was running out, which meant he had to go to the dollar store today. Linney wasn't going to be happy.

He needed to get some cereal and maybe that milk that came in cartons so it didn't have to be in a refrigerator. Linney didn't complain much, but eating cold soup and hot dogs was pretty awful.

Still, it was food. And they weren't in any old foster homes.

He moved over next to his sister. "Linney." He waited for her to stop what she was doing and look at him. When she did, he tried to make his voice happy. If he seemed happy, she'd be happy. And maybe she'd stay happy until he got back. No way he could take her with him on account of her being so recognizable, especially if she was hanging onto him. By himself, he could tuck his hair under his cap and pull his collar up high—long as it was cold out—and he just looked like another kid running errands.

"I've got to get us more food."

She nodded. She liked to eat.

"That means I have to go over to the store."

She smiled at him and started to get up. "I go, too."

"You can't, Linney. Someone might see you and take you away. You've got to stay with your lion and wait right here for me."

"I go." She stuck out her bottom lip.

"You have to be a big, brave girl and not make any noise. Remember when I used to go to the store when we lived at home?"

She nodded. "Wit' Mama."

"I didn't take too long, did I? When you were waiting for me to come back with some good things to eat, you were a good girl and you played like you were supposed to and then I was back."

Another nod. "Cookies for Linney."

"If you're really good and quiet, I'll bring you back some cookies."

"'kay."

He made his smile real and big and got one back from her. "Good girl. You go lie on your blanket, and I'll be real quick."

She picked up the lion. "Linney be good." And as he neared the loose board, she called, "Cookies for Linney!"

"Yes, ma'am."

Emerging from the barn, he checked that the coast was clear before sneaking into the woods. He stayed at its edge until he got to the road and then crossed to the dollar store. He found a carton of milk and some more cereal and the other items they needed, along with a box of vanilla wafers and two bananas.

By the time he headed back, the light was fading. He risked walking parallel to the woods instead of in them, figuring he could keep going on past the barn if anyone saw him.

No one did.

Linney was asleep when he pushed himself and his bags inside. He turned on his flashlight to see where to put things, and she woke.

"Luce?" she said quietly.

"I brought you cookies." He opened the box and tore the bag. "Want one?"

"Un-huh!"

Cookies, a half a can each of vegetable soup, and an apple for dinner. They'd live.

6 ANNIE MAC

Annie Mac stared at the stack of envelopes on her counter. She hated that pile. It would only be more bills, bills she could barely keep up with on her substitute's pay. The superintendent said he thought she might be given permanent status at the first of the year, but that "might" weighed her down with its possibility of a "might not."

With Ty not expected home for a couple of hours and Katie down for a nap, the time had come. She pulled out a chair and sat at the Formica covered table, mostly so she wouldn't collapse under the weight of bad news. Then she took out her financial planner.

The electric bill seemed inflated, but she jotted the figure on the minus side of the ledger. Cable stayed the same every month. It provided a landline, access to the Internet, and television, although she'd only signed up for the basic channels, along with PBS for its nature programs and educational shows for children. Because she budgeted well, she had the cash for those bills and her rent and groceries, but barely a penny extra for incidentals—or accidentals. She whittled away at the hospital bill left from her stint with a broken body. The hospital had been kind enough to let her pay a little at a time, but it seemed as if she'd be whittling away on it for the rest of her life.

The debit side of her finances made her fist curl around her pencil as she finished adding in these latest bills. It was Christmas. She wanted so badly to buy new things for her children, to make a fuss and decorate lavishly. If only she could get ahead and figure out how to save money.

She dropped her head to her folded arms. Ty had begged for a new bike, one that wasn't rusted. And Katie? She was old enough to learn with training wheels. But once Annie Mac wrote checks to all those dunning her, she might have ten dollars to spend on each child.

They knew there was no Santa Claus. Or fairy godmother. Or magical being to drop gifts at the foot of their bed. She'd tried to help them know that God was ever present and a help in time of need. But right now? After all those nights of praying? All those days of being grateful when recovery had begun and new friends had emerged?

She would not cry. She would not.

Soon, Ty would come racing up the stairs, and Clay would follow, his man steps trooping along behind Ty's boy steps. Annie Mac had already changed into a peach-colored long-sleeve shirt that went well with her coloring. Now she drew a brush through her hair and dabbed a smidgen of gloss on her lips—and paused mid-swipe.

What was she thinking? Who, exactly, was she trying to impress? Nothing was ever going to happen between her and Lieutenant Clay Dougherty.

If only she weren't a sucker for the smile that made her knees weak and her heart do a little flip or for the voice that could do the same thing.

She was pitiful.

Pressing her nails into her palms, she whispered to her reflection. "You really need to get a grip. Probably a life."

Fine, she had a life. And two kids. And a job. And a place to live. She was good. As long as she kept focused and, as the counselor put it, centered.

Katie wandered in from her room and held out a book. "Mommy, can we read this?"

Annie Mac looked at it. *The Lion, the Witch, and the Wardrobe.* "That might be a little old for you," she said. "See? There aren't any pictures."

Pointing to the cover, her daughter said, "That's a picture. And Ty likes it."

Which, of course, made it good enough.

"We'll give it a try."

Katie hurried to the couch, climbed up, and patted the place next to her. Annie Mac loved the story, but her eyes saw the words, and her lips spoke them, while her mind kept trying to even out her breathing. At any moment, there'd be a knock at the door.

Three pages in, there was. Katie slid down and rushed to twist the door knob. Annie Mac stood, smoothing her shirt and taking a few deep breaths to steady herself, while Katie scooted around her brother, who was first in the door, and held up her arms to Clay.

Annie Mac smiled and would have given Ty a hug, but he shifted his duffle bag and hefted it in front of him toward the living room and the chair into which he flopped, extending his legs over the bag. Exactly, Annie Mac decided, as if he were already the teen he was close to becoming. He hadn't even paused to speak.

She might as well have been invisible.

"Hey, there Katie-did," Clay said, swinging Katie up and planting a loud kiss on her cheek, which of course made her daughter giggle. "How's my best girl today?"

"We're reading the lion book. Mommy said it was too old, but it's not. It's just right." She shifted in his arms to look at her brother. "Isn't it, Ty?"

Ty glanced at the open book and nodded.

Clay set Katie back on the floor, finally smiled at Annie Mac, and held out an envelope.

"What's this?" she asked, taking it.

"Don't know. Found it taped to your railing." He angled his head toward Ty. "That boy of yours is one fine sailor. I couldn't have done the job better myself."

Ty's face glowed—at the man, not at her. "It was fun."

She fiddled with the envelope. "What can I get you?" she asked.

"Not a single thing. Ty and I had a snack, so I'm set."

"I really appreciate all you do for him."

"No need to thank me. We're pals. We happen to enjoy the same things, don't we, buddy?"

Ty grinned, nodded.

"What about next weekend?" Clay said. "I need to work on getting the Sunfish put up for the winter."

Ty turned to his mama. "Can I?"

"May I."

He sighed. "May I?"

"I thought we'd go shopping for Christmas gifts. And you both have pageant practice."

"Do I have to go shopping? You know I hate to shop."

"Pageant practice?" She hesitated.

Ty shot Clay a pleading look. Clay smiled and said, "I could take him, meet you at the church. They've corralled me to work on sets."

Annie Mac wanted to dig in her heels, but that would make her sound churlish. "Fine. I see I'm outvoted."

"Thanks!" Ty turned to Clay. "We'll get a lot of work done."

"I can help. I'm good," Katie said, releasing her thumb long enough to speak.

Clay knelt down to Katie's level. "I know you are. And I was thinking maybe one day soon you and I can do something, just the two of us. What do you think of that?"

"Yeth, pwease," she lisped around the thumb she'd tucked back in.

"You and your mama come up with a day and a time. I'm afraid you'd be bored silly with the things Ty and I will be doing. You know how guys get when they're messing around and dirty. But when it's the two of us, you and me? We'll do all sorts of fun things. Besides, we'll see a lot of each other at play practice."

Katie stared at him as her lips worked around her thumb. Finally, she nodded, released the thumb, and said, "Guess so."

"In the meantime," Annie Mac said brightly, "you and I can do something just for girls."

"Ah," Clay said. "Girl time. I've heard about that."

"Bor-ring," Ty said from his perch on the chair. He pointed to her hands. "What's that? Aren't you going to open it?"

Katie bounced on her toes. "Open it!"

Annie Mac looked helplessly at the white rectangle. Should she open it now, while she had a policeman on hand, or should she wait until she was alone?

When she set it on the table, Ty bounded up, grabbed it, and held it to the light as if that would give him a clue to its contents. "Come on, Mama. It could be something exciting. There's no return address, only your name. You gotta open it."

"I don't *gotta* do anything." She glanced quickly at Clay, but he just stood there grinning. A blush—she hated those blushes of hers—flooded her cheeks.

"Plea...se." Ty held it out to her.

"Pweese," his sister echoed.

Annie Mac poofed out a loud and very impolite sigh. "Fine. Give it to me."

She tore at the seal and flicked the sheet open. A minute later, all she could do was collapse back onto the couch.

"What, Mama?" Ty asked. "What's it say?"

She let him take the note. He read it and passed it on the Clay. Once again, her world had flipped and upended this modicum of security.

"Can they do that, Mama? Can they make us move?"

She took a deep breath. "I'm afraid so. I knew it could happen if they sold the house and the new buyers didn't want a tenant. It was always a possibility. But with the market slow, they hadn't had even a nibble in years." She leaned forward and covered her face.

Clay stepped forward. "They haven't given you proper notice, not when they're saying the first of the year. That's not thirty days. You need to call Rita. Get her involved."

Annie Mac stood and took a deep breath. "We'll be fine. I just have to start the search again. There's bound to be something out there."

Katie sidled up and grabbed the tail of her shirt. Ty was trying to be brave. She could see it in the lip he had tucked between his teeth and the hunch of his shoulders. Her kids loved living here, this close to Tadie's family and near enough to Hannah's that they could play with her dog, Harvey, any time. Moving again would devastate them.

Annie Mac turned to her son. "You need to thank the lieutenant for a lovely time."

"He already has, Annie Mac. No need to repeat it."

"Well. Okay, then. I'll thank you for all of us."

"I'll be on the lookout for a place. Ask around again." His eyes seemed to say more.

She knew exactly what that more was, but she couldn't do it. Even if it would answer her housing problem to perfection. And her loneliness problem. And her children's need of a daddy.

"Thank you. I'd appreciate it."

At the door, he said, "You know . . ."

"I do. Thank you. We'll see you later."

She took a deep breath as he left and, turning, confronted an obviously angry son.

"Why didn't you ask him to stay, have dinner with us?"

Surprised by the boy's sudden attack, she said, "I didn't think he'd want to."

"If he doesn't, it's your fault." Ty picked up his bag and stomped off to his room. "You drove him away. You always drive him away."

Annie Mac's fingers slipped up to cover her cheeks. Where had that come from?

As if she didn't know.

7 Annie Mac

A slouching Ty finally came out of his room and sat at the computer, opening one of the math games he'd downloaded. Annie Mac checked her watch. "One game, and that's all."

He shrugged, but he didn't turn around. His fingers were too busy typing. And he was probably still angry.

She'd sunk right on past angry, although not toward Ty. No, she directed her rage like darts aiming for the bulls-eye first at the realtor, then at the owners, and finally at herself. If only she'd paid more attention to that lease, she wouldn't be in this position.

Up went another prayer, where it probably got stuck on the ceiling when she looked around their comfortable little place and let the fury return. The apartment wasn't perfect. The kitchen was too small, and the bedrooms didn't give the kids much wiggle room, but it *felt* like home. They all three loved being close enough to walk to visit friends and downtown.

And now?

The phone's ring set her heart thumping, as if the caller'd read her thoughts as they slid from prayerful to murderous in less time than it took to say *amen.* Once murderous dropped in, it tugged guilt right in with it.

Annie Mac tried to wipe her thoughts clean. She'd promised—at least herself—that she'd renounce guilt, hadn't she?

Renounce. The word sat like chocolate on the tongue, leaving a sugar coat that made a person forget the bitter. *Renounce.* Like giving up a bad relationship and repudiating negativity.

Right. As if.

The phone's repeated jangling yanked her back to her messy present. She grabbed the handset, clicked it on.

It was Rita. Annie Mac tried to put a little positive into her voice. "Hey, girl."

"How're you doing?"

"Okay. I mean, I'm fine."

"You don't sound okay, and you sure don't sound fine."

"I am."

"Annie Mac."

"Yeah?"

"Talk to me."

Talk to her? Tell Rita about this latest? Rita who'd been through so much herself and yet had been there for Annie Mac all these months? How could she ask Rita for more help?

"The kids are really looking forward to the pageant this year."

"I bet they are. But, honey, that's not what put that choke in your voice."

Annie Mac covered the mouthpiece and cleared her throat. "Didn't know I had a choke in it."

"Spill. You can't fool me. We've spent too much time together for you to go telling me a lie now."

That brought a hoot past Annie Mac's lips. "A lie? I'm not lying."

"Girl, pretending everything's fine when it's not? What do you call that?"

"Keeping my counsel?"

"Well, that put me in my place." Rita's voice quieted, as if she felt hurt.

Lord, have mercy, but the last thing Annie Mac wanted to do was wound Rita's feelings. She took a deep breath, let it out, and said, "They're kicking me out of this place. First of the year."

"Oh, honey, no. Right after Christmas?"

"They sold the house. The agent, who promised to have the furnace fixed and forgot to mention this little detail when I talked to him, tacked the note to the railing. Seems the new owner doesn't want to rent. Only to own."

"I should have studied that lease for you before you signed, acted the lawyer I am. I would have made them reword it. But they should have to give you thirty days."

Annie Mac sighed. "I was so excited to get the place. And the agent told me it was a standard rental agreement."

"Well, best I can do for you now is look at it."

"I'd be grateful."

"Why don't I stop by in an hour, maybe an hour and a half? That work for you? I'm headed to Tadie's, and Martin's gone to Raleigh to see his parents. His mama is going to have a knee replacement, so he wanted to check in with her before the surgery."

"Sorry about his mama, but thank you. That would be perfect."

It would be, if Rita could use her legal expertise to get things changed back to the way they'd been, which seemed highly unlikely.

No, she'd blown it again. Made another hasty decision with which she'd have to live.

When would she learn?

Annie Mac stacked her papers when she heard Rita's knock. Katie still played quietly in her room, having a tea party with Agatha. Her soft voice came through the open doorway.

"Ty, Rita's here. You need to finish up and go in your room to read."

"Aw, Mom. I've almost won."

Annie Mac checked her watch. She'd been ignoring him, which meant he'd probably played three games, not the one she'd demanded. With a sigh, she said. "Five minutes more. Then it goes off."

She opened the door and ushered Rita into the kitchen, which opened to the dining area, which opened into the living area. "Hey, Ty," Rita called to the boy's back.

He waved without looking.

"Ty!"

"Sorry." He turned. "Hey, Miss Rita."

"That's better." And then to Rita, "What can I get you? Tea, coffee, water?"

"Water would be great. Thank you."

Annie Mac filled two glasses and joined her friend at the table. "You look as gorgeous as ever. I don't know how you manage to do that every single time I see you." She'd always admired how put together Rita seemed, her lovely features and *café au lait* skin accented by the rich colors she wore. Today she'd paired a crimson V-neck and khaki slacks.

"And you, girlfriend, look frazzled. Let me see those papers."

Annie Mac handed them over. Rita slid the original lease from its folder, read it quickly, and then perused the letter. Finally, she replaced them and took a long drink of water.

"A full thirty days' notice will buy us a little time. Remember, honey, we found this place. We can find you something else."

Annie Mac stared at the papers as if there'd be a clue magically hidden in the midst of them, some reprieve that would last longer than a month. "In spite of the fact that the furnace isn't working again, this seemed so perfect. Close to school, close to Tadie's and Hannah's."

Rita laid a hand over hers. "I bet it feels as if nothing wants to work out, but it will. Don't lose faith."

Rita said that? Rita, whose child had been killed by a man Annie Mac had brought into their life, *Rita* could show such compassion and be so encouraging? It made Annie Mac want to fold in on herself.

"You're the most amazing woman I've ever known," she told her friend. "Thank you."

Rita waved away the compliment. "Pooh. You need to know my mama better. She's the one."

"I'd like to."

"Okay." Rita stood. "I'm going to take this information with me and draft a letter to the owner's representative in the morning, including a mention of the need for heat. And we'll start looking for a new place for you. One that has a working furnace. You're going to need that soon."

"We sure needed it the night it went out."

"When that norther came through?"

Annie Mac nodded and gave her friend a hug. "Thank you. Thank you so much."

She watched Rita head down the stairs and to her car, and then she shut the door and turned out the light. All she had to do was be around Rita for an hour, and her own problems began to feel miniscule. If anyone could fix things, Rita could.

She squared her shoulders and went to play mommy to her two. Surely, she could at least be good at that.

For tonight.

8 CLAY

Clay considered himself a patient man. When you were a detective in a small town police department, you needed to be, especially when there wasn't all that much happening on a regular basis now that they'd put a major supplier out of business. Of course, another would emerge eventually, because voids liked to be filled, but if someone were here already, he was lying low and out of sight.

The county boys were busy. They'd found a dead woman in a trailer near the church Clay attended and were following leads to find her missing children. The woman had allegedly written a note saying she'd taken the children to friends in Greenville, but she didn't give any names. Sounded fishy to Clay, but until the sheriff asked Beaufort to get involved, it wasn't his business.

Times like this, Clay thought of changing jobs, and sometimes, when he faced Annie Mac and thought of the walls she'd erected around herself, he wanted to change towns. Sure, he had friends and his mother living nearby, and he had his house and creek, but having had Annie Mac and her two living there with him, having fallen for her there, sort of took the joy out of sitting alone on his deck and watching the sun rise and set—alone.

Now she needed a new home. It ought to be right on that creek. With him.

He checked his phone's calendar. Christmas was just around the corner, and he'd promised to help with scene construction for the Christmas Eve pageant. He clicked on contacts, found the number for the church office, and dialed.

When Janis answered, he said, "Good afternoon to you."

"Hey, Clay. What's up?"

"What do you know about the timing of this pageant thing? I'm supposed to help with scenery construction—though I failed to ask what happened to last year's."

"Good question," she said. "We had it stored in the barn out back, but vandals took exception to its existence."

"Really? When was that? Did you report it?"

"Sure we did. It was last spring. A deputy came out, took a look at the crime scene, and told us to put a better lock on the door. Not much more he could do really."

"Probably not. They haven't come back or done any more damage?"

"We installed motion sensor lights over the door, and the new padlock is hefty, so no, nothing else. But that's why Chuck Whitely and a couple of others have already started building new sets."

"When do they need me?"

"Any time, I'd say. Give him a call."

He left a message on Chuck's phone before checking with his chief to see if anything needed taking care of. It didn't. So, homeward for him.

He pulled in at the Food Lion to pick up some spinach and onions to go with the chicken breast that waited his attention. While he was filling a plastic bag with a slew of lemons, a cart rolled to a stop next to his.

"Hey, Clay. Buying dinner?"

He turned and grinned at Hannah. "I am. How about you?"

"Matt got a hankering for a steak. You know he's restricted, but he figures one a month isn't going to kill him."

"I imagine he's right. Otherwise, he's healthy?"

"He is. And he said he's taking me away again this year."

Clay grinned. "The man has changed."

"He has. The trip to Italy opened his eyes, let him know that travel can be fun."

"So where next?"

Hannah grinned. "Now that he's become the expert, he's decided to surprise me again."

"How do you feel about that?"

"Curious. Happy."

But he saw a sudden shadow pass over her face and remembered. He glanced around. They were alone. "Still nothing on the adoption front? I'm really sorry about that last one."

She sighed. She and Matt had had a baby lined up—until the birth mother changed her mind at the last moment. "Yeah, well, we are too. So, we're waiting. Hoping."

With that, she smiled crookedly and backed her cart out of the way. "I won't keep you. See you later."

"Tell Matt it's about time to man my grill again. Pick a nice day before it gets really cold, and we should do it."

"I'll tell him. It'll be fun to get the crew together."

"Yes, ma'am." It would, but there'd be a hole in the group if Annie Mac wouldn't join them. And there'd be awkwardness if she did.

What a mess. He should have known better. He *had* known better than to fall for her, a too-young and way-too-wounded woman.

Standing in the checkout line a few minutes later, he heard himself hailed and looked up to see Eric Houston, a new lawyer in town, just inside the door and waving at him. Thing he liked most about Eric was the man's boat. Clay grinned at himself. Boats would do it every time.

"How's it going down at the marina?"

"Not bad." Then, as Clay's few items passed from the checker's hands, Eric asked, "You got plans for dinner?"

"Nah. Just me."

"I've a new barbecue to christen and some fresh salmon to do it with. You interested?"

"Can't turn down salmon. And I've got the makings of a salad here."

"I just stopped to pick up a couple of lemons. You have enough to share?"

"I do. How about if I follow you back?"

All of a sudden the evening looked a whole lot better than it had just fifteen minutes ago. He'd met Eric one afternoon when the other man had been trying to hang onto a dock cart full of outboard on a ramp whose incline made it tricky. After that, Clay'd been invited onboard, and the two of them had talked shop—sailing shop. Clay lusted after something a bit bigger than his Sunfish, and Eric's boat, *Escape*, a 37-foot Tayana Pilothouse Cutter, looked like the perfect size. Clay hadn't wanted to stop stroking the teak. He'd lusted, all right.

Now, Eric waited on deck, ready to take his grocery bags. "Come on down below. I made sure to keep some tea on hand. Sorry it's not freshly brewed."

"Not a problem." Clay followed him down the companionway stairs to the galley. He examined the label of the proffered bottle and then unscrewed the cap and took a swig. "Not bad. Never had green tea before."

"Antioxidants." Eric pulled some baby kale from his small refrigerator. "You hankering for your spinach or some of this kale?"

"You mean like cooked?"

"Raw. I make a mean kale salad with Granny Smith apple slices, cranberries, walnuts, and a lemon juice/olive oil dressing."

"Broadening my culinary experiences. Appreciate it."

"I remember you said you like to cook. So, another thing in common."

"Absolutely." Clay grinned.

Making the salad took very little time, and while the salmon sizzled on the grill, they sat back in the cockpit, Eric with a glass of wine, Clay still sipping his tea.

A dock neighbor called out as he headed toward town. "Evening."

"I could get used to this," Clay said, leaning his elbows on the caprail at his back. "So how's work coming?"

"Still struggling to attract new clients. It'll take time."

"And your brother? You said he's why you relocated to Beaufort."

Eric moved to the grill to flip the salmon steaks. "I'm here for Hen. That's all I can say." He pointed out to the mooring field. "That old wooden boat? The one with the long bowsprit?"

Clay squinted, saw the one Eric seemed to mean. "What about it?"

"Before I got here, Henry bought her for a song. We grew up on the water, love sailing. So he's living on his and working to get her seaworthy and beautiful."

"Manual labor and keeping busy. Both good ideas. Hope you don't mind the intrusion, you know, me asking about him, but how long has he been clean this time?"

"Almost two and a half years." Eric sighed.

"Isn't that progress?"

"Yeah, but this is a new town for him, with new pressures. He's never been trusted with the role of sous chef before, especially not in a restaurant like Aqua."

"Good people there. They own Clawson's, too."

Eric grabbed a plate and the spatula. "Hen loves his job. I'm just here to help make sure it doesn't get to be too much."

What, did Eric plan to look over his brother's shoulders? Clay didn't ask, but the comparison hit front and center. Prodding someone you loved into behavior you wanted—Eric's compulsion to safeguard his brother and his own efforts to navigate the log-strewn waters of Annie Mac's fears—felt very Don Quixote-ish. Except he didn't delude himself with visions of righting wrongs (except in his job) or errant knighthood.

If only. If only.

Eric plated the fish and handed him one. "My brother's been talking a lot about a waitress he met at Aqua. She's called Agnes, except Hen said her real name is Agnese, from the Italian."

"The Italian version has a good ring to it." And the name Agnes sounded familiar. He just had to remember why.

"I wonder," Eric said, "which she looks like, the hard-sounding Agnes or the softer sounding Agnese. She's the first woman Hen has talked about since he's been here. Says she's different." He rubbed his palm across his forehead. "Guess that's what's scaring me."

"You want to tell me why? Or is it just on principle?"

"I'm Henry's trustee. There's money, a lot of it, in trust for him from our parents."

"And you think she may be after it?" Clay took a bite of salmon. He circled his fork in the air as he chewed, then said, "Delicious."

"Thanks. Can't beat grilled." Eric sipped and then set his glass down on the deck next to him. "Hen told me he's learned his lesson and hasn't said a word to her—or anyone—about the money. I hope that's true. It's not like he's flaunting what income he's allowed, not while living on that junker of his."

And then Clay remembered why he knew the name Agnes. "If I'm not mistaken, your brother's friend just inherited the big Ware house, which is tied up in a legal dispute. She has a bi-racial daughter named Brisa."

Eric's brows shot up. "I didn't know she'd been married."

"As far as I know, she hasn't."

The other man took a couple of bites, probably chewing on this new information as he ate. "Maybe that's her attraction for Hen. Maybe he wants to rescue her."

"That like him?"

"He got religion at his last recovery center. So, yeah, it's like him now."

Clay didn't say anything. From his perspective, finding God might help Henry stay off drugs.

"It worries me," Eric said. "Both the religion and the relationship. I don't have anything against Christianity, but if it turns out to be a crutch that breaks, Hen could plummet right back into the mess of two years ago."

"I get that. Have you checked out the church he's attending? The people he's involved with there? Do they have a recovery program?"

Eric shrugged. "I have, and they do."

"Maybe it's a good fit for him."

"And maybe it isn't."

9 CLAY

Clay pushed papers around on his desk, typed notes into his computer, talked to a few people on the telephone. He didn't have enough to do, which gave him way too much time to think. It irked him that he could solve Annie Mac's housing issue in a flash if only she were willing.

But maybe he was still working in rescue mode. After all, a policeman's role wasn't merely to catch the bad guys, was it? It was to serve and protect. So, he protected, and he served.

Eric saw his brother as weak and in need of protecting. Well, sure, that was understandable. And he, Clay, was the one who'd been there for his brothers and sister and mother after his father's death. He'd been the big brother, the one who worked to help his brothers through college, who moved east to be there for his mother.

Maybe it was time for him to reevaluate the attraction Annie Mac held. He'd thought he loved her, but did he love her, or, in some convoluted way, did he need her because he saw how much she'd needed him? Past tense, of course.

Yes, he loved her kids, but, again, they needed him.

Maybe if he let go of this obsession he had with Annie Mac, he'd find someone else who could and would give him kids of his own. Who'd love him fully. Whom he could love fully.

Maybe a new woman wouldn't have her fall of red hair or her almost violet eyes or her lashes. But did that matter? Did it matter if he never found another woman he wanted with a hunger that had been new to him? A hunger he'd never before experienced, not in all his forty long years? And, heaven help him, he'd probably have forty more, unless lead hit him in the gut or the heart or his Jeep failed to protect him from a madman on the highway.

Noises from the outer office, including Avery's voice as he chatted with the office manager, filtered through the open door. Avery, a junior detective who shared Clay's office, had been spending a lot of time wandering around town instead of sitting at his desk. Avery was bored.

Clay figured something would come up that required detecting. It always did, which meant this was probably only the calm before the storm. Still, he could hope the calm lasted long enough for him to enjoy Christmas Day with his family.

When his office phone rang, he picked it up. "Dougherty."

"Clay? Sheriff Bright here. I'm hoping you can give us a little help. We've got a couple of kids we've been unable to trace from out near your church. Their mother's dead."

"Out at Hinson's Trailer Park? Heard something about that."

"She seems to have overdosed. Anyway, there's some question about what happened to her boy and girl. Based on a note we found saying we didn't need to worry—like that's going to happen—we checked schools to see if children fitting their description had recently been enrolled in Pitt, Craven, or any neighboring county. Whoever they're with could be waiting until after the holidays, but I'd like to have their whereabouts confirmed so we can rule out foul play."

"You check the handwriting on the note?"

"Couldn't find a single example of the mother's to use as a comparison. She didn't have a checking account. Didn't seem to write things down. No journal. Nothing."

"Could it have been one of the kids who wrote it?"

"Anything's possible."

"What about pictures of them?"

"Only school photos. I'll fax you copies."

"Thanks. I'll get word out here. We'll be on the lookout."

"Appreciate it. I've got a deputy asking around at the boy's school. The girl has Down Syndrome and relatively severe retardation."

"How old?"

"Ten and twelve. The boy's the younger one."

Clay stopped doodling on his notepad. "Not likely to be runaways then. No ten-year-old boy's going to want—or be able—to take care of an older disabled sister."

"That's what we thought." The sheriff's voice had hardened. "Which is why we're concerned. Neighbors didn't have much to say except there'd been a man living with them about a year ago. Bobby Shafer. We're looking for him now, but there's not much to go on."

"Mind faxing me that info, too?"

"Coming up. Appreciate your help, Clay."

Clay disconnected the call. He hated cases like this, missing kids, the possibility of kidnapping. Or worse.

The fax came in a short while later. Cute kids, the boy with glasses a little too big for his face, the girl with that huge smile. Clay made copies of their photos and took one to Stella, the office manager who kept the station running.

"Will you post these please? Make sure everyone sees them. We may have two runaways from up at Hinson's. Or even an abduction." He explained the circumstances.

"Those poor children," Stella said. "I'll let everyone know."

Clay stuffed a second copy of their pictures in a folder to take with him. Christmas was a hard time of year for many people and for children in trouble? He hated imagining it.

Perhaps Ty would recognize the boy. Tomorrow was Friday and the first pageant practice. Clay'd ask around. He might get further than an unknown deputy, armed and in uniform.

After completing his reports in a two-fingered attack on the keyboard, Clay checked his watch and headed on home. The drive down east normally gave him time to unwind, but there was too much traffic today and too many thoughts hounding him.

He was supposed to meet Eric at seven for dinner at Aqua. "My treat," Eric had said when extending the invitation. "You can be my cover. Help me check on my brother without seeming to and on that Agnes woman."

Clay couldn't remember his last meal at Aqua, but he liked the place. And keeping busy was a good thing. He'd gotten used to company at mealtimes. Then he'd gotten unused to it. Two nights in a row spent in conversation? A huge plus.

He accomplished the mundane acts of arriving home, unlocking, turning off an alarm by rote. Until he entered the kitchen and pictured Ty where the boy had been, climbing on one of the stools, his hands pressed on the counter and his hair tousled, wanting to talk, man to man, saying how much he missed Harvey. "Every time I come here, it seems Harvey should be here too."

"He should," Clay had agreed. Too bad Hannah'd taken her dog back, because a boy needed a dog.

You took what you could get, didn't you? And if it wasn't what you wanted, well, too bad. Just too bad.

He filled a glass with cold water and walked out to the deck. He'd have liked to stay there, maybe watch the full moon come up off to his left, its light a wide beam on the creek. What he didn't want at that moment was to drive back into town for a dinner.

The slight chill of the north wind was merely that, a chill that hadn't had time to lower the ambient temperature by much. By the time he got to town, he wouldn't even feel it. He'd duck with Eric into the small back-street restaurant and enjoy good food. Meeting one of the chefs would also be a perk.

Perks were good.

10 Annie Mac

Practice for the Christmas pageant started at five-thirty, which meant Annie Mac had to feed everyone and get them to the parish house a little early. Besides Jilly, there'd be Agnes's daughter, Brisa, who'd begged to join them.

She bustled her two into the car and picked up the other girls at Tadie's house. "Thank you so much for doing this," Tadie said. "You're a lifesaver."

"We'll have fun. I should have them back by eight-thirty at the latest."

"You all be good," Tadie told the girls. "And buckle up."

"Yes, ma'am!" Jilly said.

Annie Mac hoped the organizers of this production knew what they were doing. At least the kids didn't have speaking parts but only had to sing with everyone and come in at the right time. And the women in charge of costumes had patterns to go by, although this year someone had donated new fabric. There would be three sewing machines available, if she counted the one in the trunk of her car.

Clay was the first to spot them as they entered the parish hall. He waved with a "Hey, all" and held out a hand to take her sewing machine. "Where do you want this?"

She indicated one of the classrooms. Katie dashed toward her friends without even acknowledging Clay.

"She's excited," he said, grinning after the child.

"I think they all are. She can't wait to don a pair of wings and a halo."

Clay laughed. "Can't blame her." And then he noticed Jilly and Brisa. "Hey, Jilly. Who's this lovely young lady with you?"

Jilly introduced them, still holding Brisa's hand. "Her mama is working so we brought Brisa."

"I met your mother when I had dinner at Aqua last night," Clay told the girl.

Ty interrupted. "Come on, guys. Let's get going."

"Hang on a minute, you three," Clay said. He set the machine on the floor at his feet and dug a folded paper from his pocket. Opening it, he turned it so they could see the photos. "Any of you know these two children?"

Ty got up close to it, stared from the boy to the girl. "That's Louis. He goes to my school, a grade ahead."

"You sure? I don't think he's as old as you are."

"Yeah, he's some kind of genius or something. He got put ahead."

"I've seen him around," Jilly said. "But that's all."

Brisa didn't comment.

"What about friends?" Clay asked. "Do you know who he hangs around with?"

"Why?" Ty asked. "What's he done?"

"As far as I know, he hasn't done anything. His mother died, and we're trying to find out where he and his sister might have gone."

"Don't know," Ty said. "You want me to ask around on Monday?"

"That would be great."

"Me, too," Jilly said. "I can ask."

"Thank you both."

Annie Mac spoke to Ty. "You and Jilly remember to introduce Brisa to Miss Joy."

"Yes, ma'am," they called, dragging Brisa between them.

"What do you think could have happened to those children?" Annie Mac asked.

Clay hefted the sewing machine again. "I wish I knew. The sheriff said they don't have a single lead."

"And it's almost Christmas."

"A hard time for children in trouble. Let's just pray they're actually with friends." Clay looked after the retreating three before heading into the costume room. "Interesting that Ty told me Brisa was more Jilly's friend than his, but it seems he's reconsidered."

"He's a boy. He's allowed to be fickle."

Clay set the machine down on the table she indicated and cocked a brow. "Not nice, Annie Mac."

She shrugged, but she could feel the heat rising even as she tried to hide a smile.

Leaning closer, he whispered, "And not at all true." Without another word, he left her to think about missing children and her own.

During the next hours, she occasionally distinguished Clay's laugh or his voice, and that little leap of something, like a spike in blood pressure, startled her. Trying to ignore the distraction, she cut and sewed and listened to the other women exchange ideas or tidbits of gossip.

Only, she didn't really hear them.

Practice ended later than scheduled, and four exuberant and probably overtired children piled into the car. The drive home was full of their chatter. Katie's class would all be angels. That was a given. And Ty already knew he'd be a shepherd. Jilly, with her bright red hair and her vivacious personality, had first wanted to play Mary and then had decided that she'd like to wear wings. "Angels get the best songs, too. And they don't have to remember as much."

"You won't *believe* what Brisa gets to do," Ty said. "Miss Joy took one look at her and—"

"And then," Jilly interrupted. "She asked if Brisa wanted to play Mary!"

Brisa's lilting voice spoke so softly, Annie Mac had to strain to hear her. "But I didn't know which Mary she meant. What she wanted me to do."

Annie Mac squinted at the road ahead. Goodness, the child didn't know about *Mary?* Hadn't she ever heard the Christmas story? "I'm sure," she said diplomatically, "Miss Joy told you, didn't she?"

"No," Ty said. "Miss Joy was too busy with everyone else. She told me and Jilly to sit down with Brisa and tell her."

"So we did," Jilly said. "And then Brisa thought she'd like to be Mary."

"It was so sad," Brisa said. "Her being forced to have her baby in a stable."

All Annie Mac could do was shoot up a little prayer for this child who didn't know what Christmas meant. Even if Brisa and her mother didn't believe, that knowledge should be part of her education. What kind of school had she attended in New Jersey?

Experiencing the pageant would be good for Brisa. She'd learn the songs, hear the story, and participate in all the fun and the magic of the season. If nothing else, by Christmas Day Brisa would know whose story they told and what Mary's role had been in it.

11 Louis

It was getting colder again, more like winter was supposed to be. Louis wished it would stay warm like last week, because now they had to huddle, sleeping in their knitted caps and their coats and gloves. There'd been frost on the ground outside the old barn that morning, and the grass had crunched under his feet.

But the cold didn't explain why today had been different for Linney, why she hadn't been okay with hugging her lion and waiting under the blankets when he'd trekked off to the dollar store for supplies. They'd needed diapers, wipes, and garbage bags, plus toilet paper, and he'd made sure she was warm enough.

Sure, the first week or so had been hard on her. She'd asked again and again and again for Mama, but she'd still done what he told her. She was a real good girl and mostly happy. Sometimes she did get stubborn, but hardly ever. When he told her to do something, she almost always did it.

Maybe he should have expected this. Sooner or later a day was bound to go bad.

Today hadn't started out bad. They'd eaten some lunch, and she'd seemed fine. He'd left her tucked in and playing with her lion, and he'd promised to come right back. "You just stay there and keep warm."

She'd nodded, but she hadn't said anything.

He'd hurried, like he always did, not taking chances. Then he'd returned to his sister so scared, she'd wet through everything, even their blankets. Now she was cold and shaking.

Good thing she wasn't a loud crier or a screamer. A very good thing. There'd been lots of cars at the church last night, and you never knew if someone was hanging around who could hear a kid scream. So he was real glad she only made little noises.

Now, he was gonna have to put his mind to work to find food without going to the store again, at least not while Linney was this upset.

He could wash her up, but no way could he wash the blankets. And no way could they sleep on peed blankets either. Then his clothes would stink, and he'd never be able to sneak anywhere.

"Wan' Mama. Wan' Baby." Her words sneaked under his skin.

He'd have liked a mama who fixed things, too.

He sat with his back against an upturned crate and drew his sister close, shushing her with soothing words, promising that everything would be okay.

Straightening his glasses, he gazed bleakly through the biggest crack, longing to be eighteen instead of ten, a man with a job who could take proper care of Linney for the rest of her life and see that she never got scared or hurt again. And because he was so scared, too, he closed his eyes and sent up a prayer to the God his mama had stopped praying to last year when Bobby'd left with curses comin' out his mouth and the stink of alcohol on his breath.

"I ain't paying you another red cent," Bobby'd screamed, "nor givin' you another thing, you—" And that's where Louis shut off the memory. He wouldn't even let himself remember the filthy words the man had used toward Mama before he'd gone on to shout equally nasty ones about Linney. Bobby didn't want to be with Mama, but calling her bad names didn't make her bad. Mama may have been real stupid about men and about how you got a kid, like she'd said, but she wasn't those things he called her. No way.

"So, God," Louis said over his sister's head. "I'm running out of ideas, you know? Mama always said Linney was one of your best Christmas gifts back in the days before she quit talking to you. I'm real sorry about that, but she was mostly sad, on account of Bobby being such a jerk and her not having very good antennae. I don't think she meant like a bug's. I think she meant she didn't know how to tell who was good and who wasn't. You probably get that." He paused and ran a hand across his sister's hair as she slept with her head on his lap.

"I'm trying to take care of your gift here, God, because I know you called me to do that. Mama always said so, said no matter how old Linney got, it would always be like she was my little sister, not my big one. She said you made brothers to take care of sisters. But it's gettin' harder. I'm still a kid. And what am I supposed to do when Linney gets even older and her body gets like Mama's?" He swallowed hard. "I guess if you want me to suck it up and do what I have to, well, I guess I will. But it kinda makes me gag, God." This time he had to quit talking for a minute to get the sour taste pushed back down. "Sorry, but I can't help it." Just the thought of what he sometimes had to do got to him.

"And I gotta be honest, if you don't mind. I really miss school. I finished that book I brought, but I'm going to get way behind if I can't figure out what's next. Besides, I don't know how to teach Linney what she needs to learn either."

Louis tried to get hold of himself so God wouldn't stop listening. He was desperate. If prayer didn't work—and Mama used to swear it didn't—then he was in big trouble. *Big* trouble.

"I don't mean to be whiny. I just figure if you're God, then maybe you've got some better ideas than I have. And maybe you'd be willing to let me know what they are?" He waited a moment. "Anyway, thank you for listening."

Linney tugged her lion close and cuddled on the stinky blanket. In the quiet, Louis tried talking to heaven again. "God? You smell that? You see how I gotta do something quick." He waited. "Any ideas?"

On that thought, he pictured the ladies he'd seen going into that church office when he'd been spying through a hole in the wall. They'd carried in boxes of what looked like food and clothes. He could tell about the clothes because they were kinda spilling out and something fell on the ground. A couple of somethings, and one was a jacket. So, maybe it was like a store in there. Maybe for the church people only, but it sure was closer than the one he'd been going to.

"I know it would be wrong to take, but I'd pay back. I promise."

He took a long, quiet breath, just in case God wanted to stop the thing he was imagining. But all he heard was Linney snuffling in her sleep. He wouldn't be gone long enough for her to wake up. Still, he asked God to keep her from knowing.

He stuffed his flashlight and a garbage bag in his pocket and crawled out of the barn. He checked around for anyone wandering near the place and then looked over at the church's office. There weren't any cars in the lot. The lady who worked there went home early most days, and the guy who wore the robes on Sunday only came mornings.

Louis kept close to the woods until he got right behind the office building. Trouble was, he was too short to reach the windows. At least there was a back door.

In movies, people hid keys under stuff, but there didn't seem to be any hiding place he could see. Without a key, he'd have to break in.

God, this is so bad.

He ducked and checked around the outside for something like a tool. His heart was doing a thuh-bub-thuh-bub in his ear so loud he figured he might be the first kid his age ever to have a heart attack.

Maybe he should just suck it up and deal with the blankets and having to leave Linney.

But what if she followed him on account of not wanting to be by herself? She could get lost. She could get hurt. It wasn't like he could go to the store in the middle of the night when she was asleep. The store wasn't open, and if she woke up after dark, she'd be so scared, he'd never calm her down again.

He had to do something, and this looked like it.

Under the stairs leading up to the church's back door, he found a long piece of metal. He'd seen one of these before, with its flat tip that worked for prying something off something else. Like prying a door open.

God, I am sorry, I'm sorry, I'm sorry.

He wondered if saying sorry before and after made it better, or if God was just gonna be real mad at him anyway. Stealing from a church seemed like the worst thing.

Only, not as bad as having Linney so scared she peed everything and everywhere.

The metal bar didn't work first try. Or second. He tried putting it in the crack of the door, but the lock was too big. He tried up the door and down the door. Nothing. The only thing that moved when he stuck the flat end in and pushed was the piece of wood outside the door. So he pushed and he pulled and he pushed some more. He heard the creak of nails sliding, so he moved the pusher up a little. More nails squeaked.

He shoulda exercised. Exercise would have meant muscles, and muscles would have helped. In between pushes on the bar he had to stop and rest on account of being so wimpy.

Some of the seventh-graders called him a wimpy geek. He knew what a geek was. He'd looked it up.

He couldn't help wearing glasses and being smart, but he could've helped being weak and skinny and wimpy. After he got them out of this mess, he'd fix that. He'd get himself some weights, and he'd start getting strong.

But not so I can steal, God. Just this once to give me time to think where to go and what to do next. How to fix things.

It took five more pushes before the piece of board cracked. Then he got to the lock thingy, turned it, and went in. His heart didn't shut up, and now he could taste stinging throw-up in his mouth.

He sucked it back, swallowed as he closed his eyes, this time praying nobody would be inside, nobody would have come without him knowing, or stayed without him seeing.

Tiptoeing into the room, he looked around. All was quiet 'cept a big clock on the wall. To the sound of its tick, he walked to the doorway and waited but still heard no one. There were a lot of rooms here, and he only wanted the place they kept the food. That was all. He wasn't after anything else. Except maybe something that could be a blanket.

And there it was, a closet with food on one side and clothes on the other. He picked and chose, searching through the bins of clothes for a few things for his sister and another sweater for him. Then, from the food, he found items that would help them get by for now.

He prayed *now* would end soon, and God would tell him what to do next. There had to be something somewhere.

An answer. *Please.*

He hadn't found a single blanket. As he sneaked back out the door, he pictured the other buildings, the church and the place kids went on Sundays. Lots of cars had been coming all week in the evenings, and people had been going in there with stuff.

Hiding the bag and the metal bar next to the back steps, he rounded the far corner of the office building and dashed across the grass to the door he'd seen people use. On the way, he made a bargain with God. If he could get in easily—no more breaking anything—he'd search for a cover. Otherwise, he was outta there.

He touched the knob. It turned. He glanced up and grinned, and then he tiptoed inside. An open door could mean someone was already inside. It could also mean they'd forgotten to lock it.

The room was big. He stood still, waiting in case he heard someone in one of the rooms off to the side. It was quiet. There was also a back hall and a sign for bathrooms. He had a sudden urge to pee at the thought of a real bathroom, but that would be dumb. He could get caught in there, and then what would he do?

So, as quietly as possible, he headed to some boards painted like sets they used in plays. In front of those was a wooden trough-looking thing that had hay in it. And behind that, hanging off one of the scenery pieces, was a blanket.

He reached out, drew the blanket toward him. And found there was more than one. With two in his arms, he began to retreat when he noticed the baby doll in that straw. He guessed that was supposed to be the manger, and the doll was supposed to be the baby

Jesus. A tear hit his cheek, and then another. The doll looked just like Linney's lost one. A perfect match.

God?

His hand had hold of the doll before he'd finished the thought, and he turned and ran out the door and around to the back of the office, where he stopped and let the enormity of what he'd done settle around him and into him and on him.

He'd stolen the baby Jesus.

Oh, he knew it was just a doll, but the church people were going to be so angry. They'd kill him if they knew he'd done it.

I'm sorry.

But as he picked up the metal bar and half-dragged the bag toward the woods' edge, his hammering heart slowed and his tears dried. And the doll in his arms felt right. Linney would smile again. She'd be happy.

All he could do was whisper, "Thank you. Thank you."

12 CLAY

The call from Father John Ames came in on his cell instead of through the office phones. "Clay, we've had some trouble here. You think you can come on out to the church?"

"What sort of trouble?"

"Seems someone broke into the office after Janis left for the day. No telling what time, but I had to get some papers for this week's homily and found there'd been a break-in. I haven't checked the sanctuary or parish house. I'm headed over there now."

"Won't take me long to get there."

Clay glanced at his watch. Maybe he could grab something to eat after he saw what had John so upset.

He pulled into the church parking lot and found John back in the office, on the phone with someone who sounded like a locksmith. The conversation didn't seem to be going John's way.

"Locksmith one, church zero," John said with a wry grin. "You know how to replace a door lock?"

The door stood wide open, and it was obvious someone hadn't messed with the lock, only the frame. "You don't need a locksmith. You need a carpenter. We'll get it taken care of."

John looked at the door again, then nodded and led him back to the storeroom where they kept items for the food bank on one side and bins of donated clothing on the other. Once a month, a volunteer sorted and took them to the appropriate charities, and if parishioners had a need, this was where they came. The bins were askew and clothing piled back every which way. "I don't have an inventory of anything, but you can see spaces on the shelves where it looks as if someone has helped himself."

"Is this all that's missing? Do you keep any money here or valuables here?"

"Not in the office. Collection money is in the sacristy safe. The safe hasn't been touched. Nor has the door to the sacristy. The sanctuary is fine. Nothing missing."

"What about the parish hall?" Clay asked.

"Joy had just gotten there when I went to check. She said the door was already unlocked. Anyway, nothing seemed out of place."

"Then I'm off to the hardware store," Clay said. "You have any tools floating around?"

Father John shook his hand.

"I'll call Matt, see if he can send someone to fix this."

"Thanks, Clay." And then the priest sent him a worried look. "What about finding out who did it?"

"To be honest, if the only things missing are cans of food and some clothes, I'm thinking you may have some homeless guy roaming the area. Maybe what you need to do is put up a sign and tell him to come around during business hours. You'll feed him."

"And I could tell him how to get to the mission in town."

Matt and another man were studying the damage when Clay showed up with new molding and a few pieces of lumber in case there were extraneous repairs needed. Clay opened the back of his Jeep.

"You know Bud, don't you?" Matt asked. "He lives out this way. Figured he'd have everything you need and be able to do the job."

"Hey, Clay. Whatcha got there?" Bud peeked around and into the Jeep's cargo section. "Good man," he said, pulling out the pieces of wood.

"You going to need help here?" Clay asked. "I'm overdue on the scenery crew, and I'm starving."

Bud waved him off. "Go. I've got this. I just finished Elma's meat loaf and potatoes."

"Don't suppose you brought leftovers."

Bud grinned at him. "Leftovers? You think we had any? Those boys of mine aren't exactly small anymore." He patted his own belly. "Then, neither am I."

"Okay, then, I'm off. I'll be a much better scene painter if I show up with a full belly." He turned to Matt. "Don't suppose we could enlist your help with this pageant?"

"And just what did you have in mind?"

"We still don't have a tree for the sanctuary. Some of the ladies have pulled folk together to decorate the one outside, like they did last year, and they've got greenery ready to go, but we need a tall tree that will show up behind the nativity scene. John said he wants one so he can link the Christmas story with the whole tree thing. Show folk who only know about the tree something about the birth of Christ, the one who, after all, spoke trees—and everything else--into existence."

Matt had his I've-got-it look. "Not a problem. If I can't find you one at a lot on my way home and have it delivered, how about I bring some boys around and we cut a good one from out back there?" Matt pointed to the evergreen woods backing the old storage barn that was part of the church property. "Look to be hollies and all sorts of pines. I'm thinking it may have once been a tree farm that gave up the ghost and went wild. I wouldn't want to take down any of the slow growers, no magnolias or even holly trees, but one of the pines maybe or a spruce?"

"You're vestry. You get whatever clearance you need. I think it would be a great idea. Besides saving the church some money."

"Isn't that the truth?" Matt said. "Can't believe what those thieves want for trees these days."

"Lots on my property, anyone needs something. Not all pretty like those back there, but they work. My brothers call them my Charlie Brown Christmas trees." That got the laugh he'd hoped for before he called a goodbye to Bud and told Matt he'd see him later.

He headed to the highway and toward the closest burger joint. Ordering took minutes, preparation a couple more. Indigestion wouldn't even take that long to kick in.

Clay sighed. He hated fast food, but at least this version had a little flavor. And the fries were great.

He washed the meal down with bottled water and headed back to the parish hall. He'd been sucked into helping this year, but he really, really longed for a quiet evening, just him and his creek with music in the background and a book in his lap.

And that was what he believed until he opened the door and saw Annie Mac and her two standing in a crowd.

13 ANNIE MAC

Ty had been the first to pull her forward to see what was happening around the crèche. He cut in front of some older boys and returned to her side. "The doll for the baby Jesus is gone."

"And two of the blankets," one of the women said. "I think they were for Mary and Joseph."

Others put forth their ideas. Brisa, Jilly, and Katie flanked Annie Mac, hands reaching for hers, clinging. The idea of someone coming into the church's parish hall and stealing may have excited them, but it frightened her.

"I heard blankets were going on the pretend donkeys." That was one of the pre-teen boys.

"Who was going to be the donkey?" said another. "You, Billy?"

"Stick donkeys, not real ones, silly." That was from one of the older girls.

Clay approached the group and laid one hand on Jilly's shoulder, one on Katie's head. "What's going on?"

"A missing doll and blankets," Annie Mac said. "Why would anyone take those? Or do you think someone just put them in another room? A prank?"

Clay cleared his throat and called for everyone's attention. He was so naturally commanding that his raised voice bought their silence. It didn't hurt that they all knew he was a policeman.

"Father John discovered someone had broken into the church office earlier today." Clay's words carried through the room. "The only things we found missing were some cans of food and some clothing, although no one knows what items exactly were taken from the donation piles. Matt Morgan's got Bud Finley over there fixing the door."

"You sure they didn't take the offerings?" someone asked. Annie Mac didn't recognize the woman. "What about the cross and candlesticks in the sanctuary or the chapel?"

"Nothing else. Except, obviously, a doll and blankets. Now, there may be other small items, and if you find anything else that's not where it ought to be, let Father John or me know." Clay paused for a moment. "It seems to us that we're most likely looking at someone who is homeless. Maybe someone hungry and cold."

"And maybe there's a kid, you know, on account of the missing baby Jesus." That was from one of the middle school boys.

"Excellent point, Jerrod. So, what I'm going to suggest is that we all keep our eyes open for someone who doesn't seem to fit or who looks suspicious. Father John would like to help whoever did this."

"Not lock them up?" That was Andrew Williams, an insurance agent who always seemed full of himself to Annie Mac.

"Of course not," she said and then glanced sheepishly at Clay. He smiled at her.

"But they broke in," said Andrew. "That's against the law."

"It is." Clay nodded at Captain Obvious. "But maybe whoever did this doesn't know where else to go for help."

"Maybe. And maybe we were just an easy mark."

Murmuring followed Andrew's words.

Clay ignored him and spoke to the group. "Report it to one of us if you see anything suspicious. In the meantime, let's get some work done. We only have a few days to go before the pageant is live!"

Annie Mac grinned at his gung-ho cheerleader's voice and spoke quietly for his ears only. "I certainly hope Andrew won't be the one to find our culprit or culprits."

"Unless, of course, the thief wasn't homeless at all but staged the robbery for some other reason."

"Yeah," she said. "Which is why he left the valuables and went for food, clothing, and a doll. Sounds highly suspicious to me."

As she worked at her sewing machine piecing together costumes, Annie Mac couldn't stop thinking about the homeless person or persons who'd broken into the church. Was there a child out there, a little girl who'd needed a doll for comfort?

She supposed the person didn't have to be homeless to be in need. He or she could just be out of work and hungry, maybe living in one of those trailers just beyond the field. Maybe the heat had gone out at their house, too. She could relate to being cold, especially at night.

Thank heavens she had the quilts she'd inherited from Auntie Sim. What if she hadn't had them? What if she and her babies were without an income, without a place to live—which could be the case come January if something didn't happen to change her circumstances. Maybe every apartment would be full, every house rented, every room at the inn taken.

There was certainly a precedent for no room at the inn. At least her name wasn't Mary and she wasn't pregnant.

And wasn't it something about Brisa not knowing the truth about Christmas? Had the child only heard about a non-existent Santa Claus whose non-existent love would never fill very real spiritual holes?

Lord, could you please work on filling some very real physical holes in our life?

She loosed a long sigh. The trouble with doing work like this, mechanical work that kept only one part of her brain engaged, was that she had too much time for the other part of her brain to fret.

She'd rented out the house she'd inherited from Auntie Sim because the thought of living between walls that had seen so much horror appalled her. Even if she were about to become homeless, its tenants had a lease, obviously a much better one than she'd gotten from her own landlord. Besides, the income from the rent paid the house taxes and insurance as well as augmenting her measly substitute's salary.

"Mama," a little voice said at her shoulder.

Annie Mac released the foot pedal to stop her machine and turned to her daughter. "What do you need, sweetie?"

"Do you think I should let them have Agatha? You know, for where baby Jesus is supposed to go?" Katie's expression suggested the idea worried her.

Pulling the child close, Annie Mac kissed the sweet cheek. "That is so kind of you, love. But I think they may want a baby doll instead of a little girl doll. I bet they'll find another one soon."

"Okay." Katie's eyes brightened. "It's just, angels are s'pposed to take care of the baby."

"Ah. Well, you do a lovely job of taking care of Agatha. And thank you for being so thoughtful."

"Okay, Mommy." Katie hugged her hard and scurried back to the other children.

That sweet baby girl.

Annie Mac wiped at her cheeks with the back of her hands. It constantly amazed her that her two loves actually functioned as caring individuals, in spite of all they'd witnessed—and experienced.

Thank you, God, for that.

Because it had to be divine, didn't it? The fact that Katie didn't remember—or at least didn't seem traumatized by—the horror of Roy. And the fact that Ty seemed to have moved past his own nightmares that had been an aftermath of the shooting.

She and Ty had talked about what had happened, and she'd asked him if he needed to speak to a counselor, too. Her boy had looked surprised. "Mama, I have the lieutenant to talk to. I don't need anyone else."

She'd been just a little hurt by that, if she remembered correctly. A little miffed that all Ty seemed to need was Clay—okay, and her. While she still hadn't moved to the other side of the whole ordeal. Or gotten past her fear that she'd made too many mistakes to want to risk herself again.

Clay walked past the open door carrying a piece of scenery that looked like the side of a stall. He wore a T-shirt, tight fitting and revealing those muscles she wasn't supposed to notice. And his jeans... Oh, man.

She turned back to the sewing machine and fed more fabric under the presser foot. She would not think about him, and she certainly wouldn't think about his muscles or . . .

Stop it! Annie Mac Rinehart, you get your mind settled elsewhere. Right now.

She grinned. She was a mess. No doubt about it, a real mess.

Tomorrow, she had a few apartments to see. Rita'd lined her up with two here in town and one just over the bridge in Morehead City.

Her children would hate relocating to Morehead, changing schools, moving far from friends. The logistics of it felt overwhelming.

But that was a worry for tomorrow. Today had worries enough of its own.

14 LOUIS

Louis waited until dark to sneak Linney out to the little bathroom. "You gotta stay real quiet. There are all those people coming into the church parking lot, and we don't want them to see us."

She put her finger to her lips.

"Good girl."

After they finished, she smelled so much better. He'd rinsed out her clothes, too, but it was a good thing she had new ones. No telling how long the old would take to dry with it so cold out.

Linney didn't care about any of it. She had a new baby.

Still, he shouldn't have stolen any of it. He knew better.

He sure hadn't planned this escape of theirs very well. He'd admit that. He'd been in a hurry and desperate to protect his sister. Because things happened in foster care, and he couldn't let her go back to that. Him either.

He'd never forget the one time they'd been in for a couple of weeks when his mama'd had to go to a hospital and there hadn't been anyone else to keep them. People had been mean to Linney. Real mean, only she couldn't tell him what they'd done. He just knew it had taken a long time to get her to calm down after they got back home, and she'd wet herself all the time for months.

Sometimes, life or maybe Linney's condition had even gotten to Mama. And then he'd have to take care of both of them, his big sister and his mama.

And at school, they'd put him in a class two ahead of his normal grade, which meant he was the only shrimp in the seventh grade. Some of the kids had been nice anyway, not all, but some. Only, not in foster care. Never there.

He sure wished he'd grow taller soon. And get some muscles.

He was sorry about the broken door on that church building. He'd figure out how to pay them back once he figured out how to get out of the mess he'd landed them in.

But it didn't look like he had an out yet. He couldn't let the social worker have his sister. And he didn't want to be in the system either. If he thought being ten and in seventh grade was hard, how would it be to be ten and living with a bunch of guys who were twice his size and real bullies? And they might put Linney in an institution this time. He couldn't let that happen.

Ever.

They'd had a close call. Nobody was supposed to be working because it was real early on Saturday, and he'd risked taking Linney to the little portable bathroom to wash her up in the water. She'd needed it. Her hair, too, which he figured would dry better in daytime. They'd been heading back across the lot to their hiding place when some guy had yelled at them.

Louis had pulled Linney along, only she wasn't real fast on account of one of her feet was a little out-pointing. It made her even more clumsy.

He hadn't taken her near the barn. Only into the woods to hide. He couldn't let anyone know they were using the barn.

Then it would be all over.

But maybe it would be anyway. If that fellow had been one of the workmen and he told, they'd lock up their bathroom. If that happened, Louis didn't know what he'd do. He sure couldn't take care of his sister without water.

15 ANNIE MAC

She'd agreed to let Ty go to Clay's again this Saturday because she had apartments to check out and really didn't want her children tagging along on this first visit. But who could keep Katie?

Tadie already had plans with her husband and children. Rita was on her way to Raleigh with Martin to see his parents. Hannah?

"I'd love to have that sweet baby come to visit. You know I would."

Yes, Hannah would. Hadn't Hannah been the first to come to her rescue after Roy? The one who'd kept her babies while she'd been hospitalized?

Annie Mac helped Katie pick out clothes for the day. "You get to play with Harvey and Miss Hannah."

Her daughter drew her thumb from her mouth and began dancing on her toes. "I love Harvey."

"I know you do. And Harvey loves you. Now hold still so I can brush your hair."

"I thought we were going Christmas shopping. We didn't get to go last week."

Only because there'd been no extra money last week. Not that she had a great deal left even now, but she didn't say that. She put on a happy face. "First Mommy has some other things she has to do. Then you and I can spend time together."

She made sure Katie had used the potty, and they were off.

Harvey dashed out the front door the moment they came to a stop in the Morgan's driveway. Barking ecstatically, he was all wiggling Irish Setter as he waited for Annie Mac to release Katie.

Hannah followed more sedately. "I'm so glad you've brought this sweet girl to spend a few hours with her Auntie Hannah."

"I'm so grateful to you." Annie Mac reached out to pet Harvey. "He seems glad to see you, Katie."

"Me, too!" She threw her arms around the dog's neck. "We're friends."

"As soon as I mentioned your name, he sat at attention at the door." Hannah leaned toward Katie. "Are you ready to come inside? You and Harvey and I can have a snack and play games."

"Ready!" Katie skipped forward with the dog.

"I'll call if I'm delayed." Annie Mac climbed back in the car.

"You go on. We'll be just fine."

Annie Mac took a deep breath, checked the map she'd printed out and the directions to her first stop, and backed down the drive.

Please, please let me find some wonderful place for us to live.

Her first stop was an apartment on the east side of town. As she pulled up to the brick buildings and found the one with a vacancy, her stomach did a flip— and not a happy one. She could never bring her children to a place like this, not with that jacked-up car at the curb and those toys scattered all over what was supposed to be a lawn. Someone was playing music loud enough for her to hear it through a closed window. Rusted lawn furniture and bikes leaned against walls in the walkway between buildings.

She picked up her phone and dialed the leasing agent. She would not be meeting him today.

The next address sounded more promising, especially as it was closer to Ty's school. She slowed as she approached, checking house numbers carefully. There it was, on the left side of a duplex. The right side housed Madame Tiffany, Psychic Reader and Clairvoyant.

Living only a wall away from a woman who read palms, looked in a crystal ball, read tea leaves and tarot cards, or pretended to talk to the dead? No thank you.

These two couldn't be the only rentals in her price range in Beaufort. What had Rita been thinking?

She turned the car around and headed out of town and across the bridge to Morehead City. She would not be discouraged. But she did dial Rita's cell phone.

Her friend answered on the third ring. "Hey, girl, have you checked anything out yet?"

"I just drove away from the first two. How did you learn about these gems?"

"Oh, are they good? Martin, Annie Mac says they're gems."

"Rita, the gem part was sarcasm."

"Oops." Rita's laugh made Annie Mac smile in spite of her disappointment. "One of the women at the center has been checking out places we might use to put some of our clients. She said they wouldn't work for us but might for you." Rita's enthusiasm had fizzled to nothing. "I take it she was wrong?"

"Let's just say, I hope you're not paying her and expecting wisdom."

"She's a volunteer. Tell me. Were they horrible?"

By the time Annie Mac had finished describing the two she'd seen, Rita's laughter had Martin begging for an explanation. "In a sec," she told her husband.

"I'm headed over the high rise bridge now," Annie Mac said. "I'll let you know what I find at this last one."

"We're almost to Raleigh," Rita said. "I'll call you later, and you can tell me you found the perfect place."

"Hope so."

The directions took her down Bridges for a couple of miles before she had to turn right, then left. The houses grew progressively smaller as she drove. When she finally located the address, she pulled into the driveway and stared at a tiny Cape Cod, painted a soft yellow. It was tidy with well-kept hedges and even a porch swing. And the neighborhood wasn't bad at all. She could imagine them living here. She really could.

With a smile, she walked next door to get the key from someone named Tallent. A slightly stooped older lady opened the door before Annie Mac had even knocked.

"I've been watching for you," the woman said. "I have the key right here. I put it on the table when that young couple returned it an hour ago because I wanted to have it ready. They were a delightful couple and really liked the house, so you may be too late, but you're welcome to take a look at it for yourself in case they change their mind."

"I'm too late?"

"They were going to call the owner. I told them they weren't the only ones coming to see the house today."

"Ah." Of course she'd be too late.

"Would you still like to take a look around?"

"Yes. Thank you." It wouldn't hurt to see it, and maybe the couple would find something more to their taste. And maybe she'd discover it was in terrible shape and not a place she'd want at all.

It was perfect. A little cottage with three bedrooms and a den, as well as a living room and a kitchen twice the size of the one she had now. And the back yard already had a swing set.

She reluctantly returned the key to Mrs. Tallent and said she'd call later. The older woman nodded. "If it's supposed to be yours, it will be."

Annie Mac tried not to hope that "meant to be" would be "meant for her."

Hannah wanted to keep Katie with her while they ate peanut butter sandwiches. "You come fetch her later, okay?"

That was fine with Annie Mac. She had shopping to think about and how she'd pay for Christmas gifts for all the good people in her life. If her permanent posting at the school didn't come through, she was going to have to reconsider teaching. Or she'd have to augment her salary with another job.

And then who'd take care of her babies?

One foot in front of the other. That was all she could do. Move forward and pray/hope/try to trust that a solution would come before she and her children found themselves sitting on the sidewalk, homeless.

"That won't happen." She spoke the words vehemently to her car's windshield. It wouldn't. Not on her watch.

And now she was talking to herself.

She returned to the apartment that was still hers and climbed the stairs. As she made herself a toasted ham and cheese sandwich, she tried to imagine what she might be able to find at the dollar store. She couldn't shop on Front Street, even if every time she passed Down East Creations, she longed to go in and buy just one thing. Maybe one of Hannah's mugs to replace the chipped pieces in her cupboards, rummage-sale items she'd bought to replace what Roy had destroyed.

If only she were talented like Hannah, the potter, or Tadie, the jewelry maker. Or brilliant like Rita, whose lawyerly expertise helped so many.

If only.

Oh, *stop it.* Pity parties were the *worst* things.

She worried the issue as she ate her sandwich and washed the pan, as she dried it off with care as if it might hold the secret to a brilliant strategy.

Maybe it did. When she bent to tuck it in the cupboard, her gaze fell on her bread pans. And she squinted as an idea took shape.

She could bake gifts. She knew how to cook. She liked to bake.

That thought put a smile on her face. Auntie Sim's apricot bread would be a treat. Lots of fruit and nuts.

Why not? One for each of her friends.

For the first time that day—no, for the first time in weeks—she began to believe in possibilities.

16 CLAY

After a day of hanging out at his house, Clay'd brought Ty with him to the church an hour early. They were about to go inside when Hannah Morgan showed up with her husband, Matt, and with Bud, who'd not only fixed the office door but had brought a chainsaw to cut a tree from the woods. *And* they'd found what looked like some kind of pine, full and certainly big enough to impress congregants.

"Wow," Ty said. "That's some tree."

Bud stood it upright. "Looks like either a white pine or a Virginia pine. Not sure."

"Gorgeous, isn't it?" Hannah asked.

"Sorry it took me so long to get things together and the tree cut," Matt said.

"You got it here in time and before we set up the scenery," Clay said. "That's all that matters."

"Who's going to decorate it?" Hannah asked.

Clay tried to remember if he'd heard anyone say. "I don't really know. One of the women's groups took care of the outside tree and all the other decorations. We could ask Janis, only she's not around today."

"They have enough lights?" Matt-the-fixer asked as he studied the tree. "It's going to take a lot if John wants it to make a statement."

"Look," Clay said. "I don't know anything. But I'm positive no one will mind if you guys want to take on the project and do with it whatever you want. It would be great if there were lights hung before service tomorrow."

Hannah looked pleadingly at her husband, who raised both brows, pursed his lips, and finally nodded. "Okay!" she said, exultant. "Clay, you tell Bud where to put the tree, and Matt and I will go buy lights."

"Bud? You okay with that? I'll help you haul that thing. And Ty here will give us a hand."

"You just lead the way," Bud said. "I'll hang around to help with the lights, soon's you two get back," he told Matt.

Clay and Ty helped Bud carry the tree through the double doors and carefully down toward the front of the church. Clay paced off the area where a couple of stable walls would be erected and then called Bud over.

"We need it visible from the back, but not in the way of the rail or the sets that will go up after service tomorrow. What do you think?"

Bud walked around, looked at it from all sides, and said, "Here." Then he brought in the tree stand, set it on plastic Clay laid down, and together they fit the tree in. "Good job," Ty said.

Clay hid his smile. Good job indeed.

"I'll neaten up around it here," Bud said. "There's a ladder somewhere, isn't there?"

"Parish hall, back closet."

"Good. I'll have it ready when Matt and Hannah get back. See what we can do to make that tree look festive."

"Thanks," Clay said. "Ty and I'd better get over to the parish hall and to work."

The kids—and participating adults—had two more practices. Tomorrow, the scenery would be set up in the sanctuary. On the twenty-third, they'd have the dress rehearsal, and then it would be Christmas Eve and the moment they'd been waiting for.

Clay followed Ty, but something caught his eye back in the direction of the woods.

Look at that. Two kids walking hand in hand. He wondered if they'd come from the trailer park. This time of year, the woods were navigable. He used to love to wander on his family farm and find animal tracks or a place to make a fort.

He hoped if those two belonged to the trailers, they'd come for the Christmas Eve service. It was open to the entire community, of course, and he'd seen flyers in the local shops. Maybe their parents would even bring them.

You didn't normally see a boy and girl that age holding hands. Kind of sweet, really.

But as they disappeared among the trees, his thoughts slid to the two missing children who were still unaccounted for, according to Sheriff Bright.

What if?

"Be right back." He spoke over his shoulder, not waiting for Ty's response.

He scanned the area as he dashed toward the woods. He was still searching when Ty caught up with him.

"What's going on, Lieutenant?"

He was too late. The pair had vanished. "Nothing. Let's head on back." The niggling suspicion that he should keep looking warred with his conviction that those two had already made it back to the trailer park.

"But you were running."

"Oh, I saw two kids wandering out here. Thought I'd catch up to them and ask if they knew anything about the missing children." He discarded the unlikely possibility that they had actually been Louis and his sister. No, those kids were just locals.

In a very few minutes, the parish hall and adjoining classrooms would be filled with kids and adults getting ready for the big day. He, instead, was itching to do more detecting and a whole lot less Christmas-pageanting.

But no way would he ever want to miss Ty and Katie's big performance. So, he studied the chaos of things yet to be painted and let out a sigh. Good thing no bad guys needed catching this afternoon.

Only a petty thief who might or might not be homeless. And two missing children who might or might not be safe.

Clay was coming out of the bathroom when he spotted Ty heading toward him wearing his shepherd garb. "What d'you think?" the boy asked, hooking his fingers in the rope at his waist.

They were alone in the hallway. Clay braced one hand on the wall and cocked his head to check out the newly constructed costume. "Yep, you look exactly like a shepherd. Just need a few sheep."

Ty mimicked his position, but he couldn't hold it—or stand still. "And a dog. Dogs are good with sheep. Do you think the shepherds back then used dogs?"

Clay pretended to consider that. "That's a great question. I wonder if there's a way we could find out?"

"You never see dogs in the pictures, do you? But why not? Didn't they have dogs?"

"I bet they did. Why don't you do some research and let me know?"

Ty grinned. "I could. We have that computer you gave us last year."

"Glad it's getting used, but I'm not going to sleep easily until you find out about Holy Land dogs and fill me in."

"You think they were holy dogs?" At first Ty only grinned, but he found his own joke so funny, he broke into a full-on laugh, falling back against the wall.

Clay waited for the laughter to die. "That was a good one."

"Holy dogs..."

"You find any, you let me know."

When he finally sobered, the boy said, "Sir?"

Clay'd been about to turn away, but that stopped him. "Yes, son?" Using the word brought about the same quick heart twist it always did.

"You still going to Raleigh on Christmas?"

"I told them I would. What about you? What are you and your mama and Katie going to do?"

"I don't know. Mama hasn't talked about it much since she got the letter about having to move."

"Has Miss Rita been helping her with that?"

"Yeah. She said she'd write the man a letter. I don't know what happened then."

"Are you worried about it? About where you'll live?"

"Kinda." Ty balanced one foot against the wall and hung his head. When he looked up, his eyes were damp. "I wish we could live with you."

Clay laid a hand on the boy's shoulder. "I know. I do too. But your mama doesn't want to."

Ty cleared his throat. "You know she wakes up screaming some nights?"

That got Clay's attention. Screaming? "You think she's having nightmares?"

Ty nodded. "Yeah. Sometimes she talks in her sleep. And she's not so quiet, so I know. She's thinking about Roy."

Clay released a huge sigh. Maybe that was the root of it. Her inability to let it all go.

Could it be that simple?

"Thank you for telling me." He straightened and pulled the boy close. He could hear voices coming from the main room, so he made the hug quick and hard.

This new information made him take another look at his own motivations. Hadn't he wanted to give up on loving her? Thought about it, because it seemed she'd never get past her fears to let him in? Even imagined that his love for her might stem from her neediness and his desire to fix things?

He had.

If only she could get her life on track. Find a permanent home, a permanent job, a permanent feeling of safety. If she were strong and independent, maybe she'd let him in, because he already knew his feelings for her had nothing to do with her need and everything to do with his.

He looked the boy in the eye. "I love you and I love your mama. We'll figure this out."

Hope sprang to Ty's eyes. "Promise?"

"I can't make miracles happen, but I promise to keep on loving you all and to keep on praying. You pray, too. After all, this is the season of miracles, isn't it?"

Ty's grin exploded. "It is! Yes, sir. I'll pray extra hard for a miracle." And he stuck out his hand to shake Clay's. "It's a deal."

Ty left him then, hurrying back to join the others for practice, and Clay headed off to see if he needed to help with anything else before he headed home. Alone. To his empty house.

Which he loved. On the creek he loved.

He hated the thought of Annie Mac and the kids spending Christmas alone.

With that thought in mind, he headed toward the costume room. Annie Mac sat on the floor, pinning up a hem for one of the angels. She glanced up when he walked in.

"How're all you ladies doing?" Clay asked.

Annie Mac smiled around lips clamped down on a couple of straight pins. The others called out a "fine," a "great," and an "almost-done."

He stooped down on his haunches near the child in the costume. "Look at this lovely little angel. Don't you look . . . angelic?"

The child beamed at him. "Pwetty?"

"Very pretty. Beautiful."

She reached over to give him a hug, almost knocking him off balance. "You're welcome," he said as he hugged her back.

Annie Mac finished and told the child to take off her costume so she could fix it. "Behind that curtain, honey. Put on your own clothes." The child just stared at her. "Can you do it by yourself?"

"Un-unh."

"I'll take her," one of the other mothers said.

"Thanks, Sylvie."

Clay stood to help Annie Mac to her feet. "Ty just asked me about Christmas Day. He said y'all don't have plans."

Her expression became guarded. "Ty asked you? Why would he do that?" She didn't look at him, but kept her voice lowered for his ears only. "You don't need to worry about us. We're not your responsibility."

He heard, all right. She'd drawn that line, hadn't she, one he kept tiptoeing across just so she could slap him back. Stupid of him.

He turned without saying another word. On the way to his car, he tried to smile at those he passed, but he doubted his lopsided effort fooled anyone. It certainly wouldn't have fooled the always alert, never-to-be-his-son Ty, who'd watched him leave the sewing room and whose gaze, Clay was sure, followed his ungainly walk of shame from the parish hall.

His bad leg hardly hurt most days, and his limp had evolved to barely there. Until moments like this, when eyes would have been on his back, and he'd have wanted to strut confidently forward.

Well, that wasn't happening. As far as he could tell, not much good was happening in his life, certainly not today, not this month, and not this year.

He wondered if Eric was sitting alone on his boat. Too bad Clay wasn't a drinking man, a guy who could take a six pack and share a few with another guy.

Then again, Eric might have a date all lined up. He was a good-looking man. And successful. And he had a great boat. Probably had women knocking on the boat's topsides, asking for a tour.

Clay pulled open the heavy Jeep door and climbed behind the wheel. Swallowing the sour taste that had inched up his throat, he shifted into reverse, backed out, and set the car to forward and the long drive home.

He tried to shush the voices clamoring for attention in his head by turning on the radio. The talk station had some argumentative moron calling in while the host didn't sound much better. He hit the change-channel button on his steering wheel, but the classic music station was having a fund-raiser. The rock station screeched. The country station was playing something with a bit of pep and some okay lyrics, so he left it there. And then the next song decided to tell him how unfaithful all women were, which he didn't actually believe true, so he hit the Off button.

Which left only the noise of the tires on asphalt and the sweet sound of a well-tended engine to drown out reminders of his stupidity. And the horrible awareness that he was a fool, and a self-pitying one at that.

He'd didn't need this in his life. He'd been fine, and he'd be fine again. All he had to do was put himself out there and find someone new. He might not have been as young or good-looking as Eric, but he'd never found women running from him before. Give his family the go-ahead, and they'd have women lined up for his inspection by the next week.

He wasn't quite ready to go that route yet, but it was past time to start protecting himself. Best thing he could do was skip the next practices and dress rehearsal, go to the program on Christmas Eve, and then head directly from that service to his sister's house. Christmas would be great. His family—his real family—would all be together, and there'd be cheer and blessings and great food. And in about three months, he'd be the uncle of a little girl, who'd be beautiful and happy because she'd be surrounded by so much love.

And he'd add to it, as best he could, all the days of her life.

Too bad he'd promised Ty never to give up on his mama. A promise was a promise—unless it became an impossibility. And then it was merely a regret.

17 ANNIE MAC

On the way home, all four children vied with each other to talk first or loudest. "One at a time," Annie Mac said.

Brisa, who seemed to have adapted to her role as the Savior's mother, said, "I get to put the baby in the manger, carefully and slowly, so everyone can see and like it."

"I bet you'll do a great job," Annie Mac said. "Are you all learning your songs?"

"Yes, ma'am. They're real pretty," Brisa said.

"I already know most of them," Jilly said.

Ty kept quiet. She supposed Katie was sucking her thumb.

After they dropped off Jilly at her house and Brisa just up the street at hers, Annie Mac took her own two back to their very impermanent apartment for which she trusted there'd be a replacement very soon. Now that school was out for the holidays, she'd have time to search.

Ty led the way up the apartment stairs, waited for her to unlock the door, and then hurried inside and plopped down on the couch. Annie Mac tried to sound cheerful. "You two want some hot chocolate?"

"Yeah." Ty scrambled up. Obviously, whatever was bothering him didn't affect his ability to appreciate drinkable dessert.

"Me, too!" Katie said.

A simple treat, a bonding moment. After all, she'd been so busy all day, and Ty had been gone, and the hot milk did seem to negate the effects of chocolate.

"How was your time with the lieutenant?" she asked him after turning on the burner under the pan of milk.

"We cleaned up the shed and got the sailboat put away for the winter. Mr. Clay hangs the boom and mast and the sail up in the rafters with lines so they don't get on the floor and the critters don't make nests in them. And he has a special shelf for the daggerboard and rudder. It's neat. He's real organized."

"Lovely." She concentrated on stirring the cocoa into the milk so it wouldn't burn.

"He says when it comes to boats and tools, everything's got to have a place and everything's got to be in its place."

"That's a good rule. I like my kitchen that way."

"Yeah." But she could hear in Ty's silence the hope she wouldn't say anything more.

She couldn't waste the opportunity. Why would she? "Don't you think all rooms should be like that? With our toys and books and clothes put away where they belong?"

"Sure. I guess so." But he was looking at his sneakers instead of at her.

"Get the mugs down, will you?" The milk was hot, but not boiling.

Katie tucked Agatha under her arm as she slid onto a chair. "Angels gotta be there tomorrow right after church. It's 'portant."

"Is that tomorrow's practice time?"

"We get to have lunch first," Ty said. "Then come back."

Well, it looked as if tomorrow would not be a day of rest. Although, did a day of rest actually exist for a mother who had to find a new home and enough money to take care of her children?

Annie Mac was surprised to see Brisa and her mother follow Tadie's crew into church the following morning. Maybe Agnes had come to make sure her daughter wasn't involved with crazies.

First Tadie, then Agnes nodded to her as they followed Brisa, Jilly, and Will with Sammy toward the front. Will slid in next to Clay, and the others followed. Annie Mac stayed near the back and glanced at her two when worship started. The children would all head to Sunday school before the liturgy began, and she'd be sitting back here, among virtual strangers, while her friends all seemed to have congregated in front.

She did her best to concentrate through the sermon and after the children returned, but she found herself checking out the way Agnes seemed to glance over at Clay a few too many times, and how the other woman—and her daughter—seemed to watch him as he and the others slid past when it was their turn at the communion rail.

Annie Mac pulled her wandering attention back and tried to refocus. Communion wasn't something she should take lightly. It certainly wasn't the time to harbor ugly thoughts.

She tossed up a prayer and hoped it covered her.

At the end of service, Ty poked her and pointed out the huge tree at the right of the altar, brilliantly lit with white lights. "I helped the lieutenant and Mr. Bud bring it in. Isn't it humongous? Miss Hannah and Mr. Matt brought the lights. They worked with Mr. Bud to have them ready for today."

"The tree is magnificent."

"I wish ours was big," Ty said. "And real."

She agreed on the real part. But she couldn't afford more than the plastic model she'd set up last week.

When Tadie came out with Sammy on her hip and the others—minus Clay—right behind, Annie Mac said, "I'm going to take my guys for barbecue before bringing them back for practice. You want to join us?"

Tadie glanced around at Will and Agnes. Will said, "Our treat. For everyone."

"Oh, you don't need to do that," Annie Mac said.

Tadie waved away her scruples. "Annie Mac, you're doing the driving for all of us. Let us treat you, for heaven's sake. And, Agnes, you're our guest."

After a quick and rather hectic lunch, the kids crowded into her car, belted in, and waved goodbye to their parents. Annie Mac had alterations to finish for some of the costumes. The other women would be working on props, such as wings and haloes. The kids would be practicing their songs, and sets would be moved to the sanctuary. They had a busy afternoon ahead.

Clay didn't show up. Maybe he had bad guys to catch. Detecting to do.

Of course, when he wasn't at the remaining practices or even the dress rehearsal, she bit her cheek, told herself it wasn't her fault, and felt wretched

But wretched only extended to her non-existent love life. On other fronts, things started to look up.

With school out, she was busier than ever—or so it seemed, baking and cleaning, wrapping the small gifts she'd bought to go in the kids' stockings, entertaining them, chauffeuring the crew to practice.

She'd been horrified when she'd shopped for baking supplies and the cashier had tallied her bill. The cost of apricots, raisins, and walnuts had her reeling. She could have bought everyone Christmas CDs for less.

But these would be from her own kitchen, made by her own hands. And so she baked, and wrapped, and labeled, and baked some more.

And then on Wednesday afternoon, two things happened that changed not only her attitude, but also her immediate future. The first came as a call from the principal of her school. He'd finally gotten the okay to hire her to a permanent position as a fourth-grade teacher. "Merry Christmas," he'd said.

Merry Christmas indeed.

She'd barely had time to digest this good news when Rita called. "Honey, you'll never guess. I just received an answer to the letter I wrote asking for an extension for you to move out. They're not just giving you thirty days. You have until the end of January to vacate!"

Annie Mac fell back into the nearest chair. "All month?"

"Yes, ma'am. I laid it on about how long it took to get the furnace fixed, and they probably figured you'd sue."

"Did you threaten them?"

"Of course not," Rita said. "I just mentioned your two young children and their responsibility to provide a functioning furnace."

It was all too much to take in, and Annie Mac had to bite the side of her cheek to keep her emotions in check. "This is so much more than I imagined. Especially because your news is not the only good thing I've heard today."

"Tell me."

"Oh, Rita, I'm now officially a full-time teacher."

Rita's shriek made Annie Mac laugh. "Girl! You rock!"

"I know. Think about it. Think how much more money I'll be making."

"Today is your day," Rita said. "And that will open up so many more housing possibilities."

"Hang on. I'm not going to be rich. Teachers are grossly underpaid."

"Oh, I know that. But your salary will be a whole lot more than you're making now for doing the same work. It's about time they did this."

"I've thought so since August." Annie Mac sighed. "Anyway, you're right. I can afford more and better, maybe even one with new appliances. I'd love not to have to scrub around nicks in the kitchen sink and stare at stained counters."

"That's it. This is why the house in Morehead didn't work out. It may have been a cute place, but it wasn't where you wanted to be."

"It wasn't, was it?"

"Right after the holidays," Rita said, "you and I will go looking. And we'll find the perfect place for you to rent."

"Thank you. Thank you so much."

"We'll see you Christmas Eve. You tell your sweet ones we'll be there cheering them on."

"I'll tell them."

Annie Mac clasped her hands over her heart. Christmas had indeed come to the Rinehart home. She had choices now, didn't she?

She was a fully employed woman who actually had choices.

18 LOUIS

Tomorrow was Christmas Day *and* Linney's birthday. He needed a gift for her. No matter if they were here, in hiding. She wouldn't understand if she didn't get something.

Of course, all she said she wanted was a tree with lights. He'd made her a kind of funny pretend tree from a pine branch he'd dragged inside the barn. He'd stuck it in one of the empty cans and braced it against a barrel, only he didn't have lights for it. Or any pretties, as Mama called them. So it was just a branch. It would never be a tree.

"Like 'at one," she said, pointing to the brightly lit tree outside the church. She could only see it through the hole or by peeking around the corner of the barn once it was dark outside. She couldn't touch it or get close enough to see it well. Especially without her glasses. She'd had some, a long time ago. But somebody'd stepped on them, and Mama hadn't been able to take her for new ones.

Of course, Mama'd gotten him a pair, for school she'd said. He had glasses that worked. Linney squinted her already squinty eyes.

He worried about her ears, too. Sometimes he had to repeat things, and sometimes she cocked her head so her left ear was closer to him, like it worked better than the right. When he figured things out for them, when he found them a safe place and a way to get more money, first thing he'd do was get somebody to make Linney new glasses and to test her ears.

For now, he had to figure out a Christmas birthday present that would help her forget about having her own tree. Mama used to set up a fake silver tree with a few ornaments and a small string of different colored lights. It always sat behind the couch on a messy table—except the times Mama'd been okay enough to clean. After Bobby left, she'd pretty much quit trying, so Louis had put up the tree last year and had done his best to straighten up the trailer. Last year, Mama'd told him to get enough dollar bills from her jar to get himself a gift. Linney, too. He'd bought the baby doll.

"What'd you get yourself?" Mama'd asked, probably counting how many dollars he'd had to spend for the doll and how much she'd said he could take.

He'd told her he was fine, didn't need anything. She'd lain in that bed, and tears had wet her hair and pillow. "I'm sorry. Just so sorry."

He could remember standing there, hanging his head because he couldn't fix her. "It's okay" was all he'd been able to say.

This year, Mama was gone, and all Linney had was him. If he was going to get her a present for tomorrow, he had to go out today. Everything would be closed on Christmas Day.

But how could he leave her? If he did, and she got upset, would it be worth it? And really, would she even remember that tomorrow was Christmas and her birthday?

No, not unless he mentioned it again. So, he could just keep quiet and pretend it was any old day.

The image of the church and the people who'd been coming every night filled him with uncertainty. If she looked out or if they went to the bathroom, she'd see the tree and see the people, and she'd know. Christmas was special enough that a person couldn't hide it.

And if she knew it was Christmas, she'd know it was gift time. She could hold onto ideas once she'd learned them, and she'd sure learned that one.

Keeping track of what she remembered and what she didn't could make a guy crazy, but she'd figured out how to match up her birthday with Christmas and a gift. Maybe she didn't know what a birthday was exactly, but she got the idea of one day, one gift.

Mama used to say too much stuff would just confuse Linney, but with one thing to play with, she'd be happy for weeks. With her baby doll, she'd been happy for a year, until she'd lost it.

Louis whispered his thanks. "That new baby made her real glad, God. You know, your doll."

And Linney's happiness made the stealing of it not feel so awful, even if he did get in trouble for taking it. Getting in trouble and paying back were owed. But maybe when he told, the church people wouldn't be too angry. Only, he couldn't tell yet. Not before he figured things out.

Maybe, just maybe, he could sneak to the store while it was still light—if he could get Linney to sleep. He could run to the dollar store real quick and get back before she missed him. She'd be safe. Nobody knew they were here.

To start, he'd feed her. He opened a can of baked beans and a box of crackers. Cold beans were okay, and maybe a full stomach would make Linney sleepy.

He ate some of the beans and then passed the can to Linney so she could finish the rest and not have to worry about passing it back. "It's all yours. You eat it all. And here are some crackers for you. Your pile. Right there."

Then he poured water into her cup and some into his, and they munched on a few salted crackers that were kind of stale.

"You finished?" he asked when she handed him the empty can.

"Un-huh."

"Then go get Baby. You both need a nap. Okay?"

"'kay."

He helped her settle. Then he said, "I'm gonna go out for just a few minutes. You go to sleep, and when you wake up, I'll be back, and we'll go get washed up. How does that sound?"

"No. Stay."

"I'll stay while you go to sleep. I'm just telling you so you won't worry if you wake up. I'll be right back. You won't even miss me."

"Stay." Her face started to scrunch up.

"Lie back down. Come on, be a good girl."

With a sigh, he smoothed her hair away from her round face and tried to remember a song, any song, Mama used to sing. He settled on one he'd heard coming from that church the other evening. "Si-i-lent night, ho-o-ly night, all is . . ."

Soon, Linney slept, and he sent up a prayer for God to watch out for her while he was gone. He took some more bills out of his dwindling stash and then ducked out the broken board.

It started to snow as he made his way into the woods and out to the road that ran along the property line. Nobody was working the site today, on account of it being Christmas Eve, but he knew the store would be open.

He shivered and pulled his jacket collar up high as it would go, hunching into it.

He could only buy what he could carry in the plastic sacks they gave him, so he shopped carefully. It was a good thing the people behind the counter weren't bright or aware of much and didn't seem to think it strange that he bought odd stuff for a kid.

He collected what he and Linney needed and found a pretend baby bottle she might like, along with a bright book of colored animals for a dollar. Then he paid and headed back across the snowy highway, careful now so he wouldn't slip.

By the time he was close enough to see the church, the parking lot had filled, and lights blazed from inside and out. A yearning hit him so hard that at first he didn't know what to do with it, and all he could do was stare.

If only they could go into that place tonight. Feel the warmth, listen to the songs he knew they'd sing.

God?

Louis passed his bags inside first, trying to be quiet in case Linney was still asleep. He climbed inside, turned on the flashlight, and set it so he could see to put things away, cans with cans, diapers with diapers, new flashlight batteries in their own space. He tucked her gifts toward the back.

She still hadn't awakened when he turned toward her, keeping the beam of light away from her eyes. Her blanket was empty. He shined the flashlight around the barn. She wasn't here. He called her name. Nothing.

Panic hit, hard and fast. "Linney!" Had she wandered toward the road? Come looking for him? Fallen in the woods?

He carried his flashlight now, shining it on the ground outside. He prayed there'd been enough snow before she'd left for him to find tracks.

At first, all he saw were his own. And then he noticed something that made him cold all over. Really cold. Really sick and scared and ready to scream and hit almost anything, because there were two sets of footprints, one that had to be his sister's and another belonging to what looked like a man. A big man.

Louis ducked back inside and found the long piece of iron he'd used to break into the office. He carried it in one hand and the flashlight in the other, and he crawled back out and began to go after them.

O, God. He'd heard what bad people could do to girls. It wasn't a secret where he came from.

Please help her. Please send angels to save Linney.

He begged and he pleaded and before long his tears were probably freezing on his cheeks, but they wouldn't stop, and he couldn't stop, and his glasses kept fogging. The footprints went into the woods and kept disappearing where trees had kept snow from sticking to the ground. He'd find the tracks again and press forward, and then they'd be gone again. His heart slammed against his ribs, almost breaking them, almost making him topple over.

Once, he did fall to his knees. So he stopped there, in spite of getting wet, and he listened. But he heard only his own breaths coming hard and fast.

At least he hadn't heard a scream.

19 LINNEY

The bad man hurts Linney, pulls hard. Linney wants him to stop. The dark woods scare her.

Luce. Linney needs Luce.

The bad man says bad words. Linney knows those words. *He'd* said them. Then he had gone.

Mama cold. Mama gone. Only Luce for Linney.

Linney's foot hits tree. She starts to fall. Bad man pulls. Says more bad things. Pulls more. Hurts Linney. Keeps making her go away from Luce.

Feet go fast. Too fast. Man looks back. Pulls. Hurts. Falls. Man stays on ground.

But Linney has her hands. She waits.

Not long. Not here.

And then Linney runs from the dark.

From man. From bad.
To lights. To tree. To Luce.

20 ANNIE MAC

Snow brought magic to Christmas Eve in Eastern North Carolina. It had started falling even before they arrived at the church. Now, as they walked from the parking lot to the parish hall, Ty tried catching snowflakes in his mouth, and Katie giggled and wiped flakes from her eyes.

The pageant seemed to have brought out everyone, filling the building with friends and family of those participating, along with those who didn't want to wait for the midnight service. There was magic, too, in the tree and the lights, the candles everywhere, the greenery. And, oh, the new sets were perfect.

Everything was perfect.

Annie Mac helped the children dress in their costumes and line up with their teachers, and then she found a place to sit next to Rita and her husband Martin in waving distance of Hannah and Matt. Agnes sat with Tadie again. And there was Clay a couple rows up from where Annie Mac sat, some new man on his right side. A handsome man, maybe in his thirties. She wondered who he was, of course. Who wouldn't?

The sanctuary was filled with excitement as people waited for the musicians to begin the service. They'd lead the young voices as the pageant unfolded.

She looked again at the tree with its hundreds of tiny white lights winking brightly. Hannah and Matt never did anything halfway. She glanced over at them. Hannah laid her head on Matt's shoulder for a moment, and he leaned toward her.

And then the music began with "Angels We Have Heard on High," during which the sweet young angels moved in to stand on a platform, the youngest and smallest below the taller ones. Her baby stood proudly among them, singing along as best she could. Between songs, congregants would read from the Book of Luke. After the first passage came "O Come, O Come, Emmanuel." The beauty of the carols always made Annie Mac want to weep.

She wasn't sure what made her turn toward the window. Snow fell on the girl's nose, on her hair, on her cheeks as she pressed close to the glass with such a look of longing. Someone had to bring that child in from the cold.

Annie Mac nudged Rita, pointed, and whispered, "I'll go get her."

She glanced once more at the front, where the shepherds, including Ty, were entering to "Away in a Manger." As she pushed through into the narthex, Clay just behind her, she prayed Ty hadn't seen them leave. But surely he'd understand when he knew the reason.

They approached the girl cautiously, and Annie Mac spoke gently. "Honey, aren't you cold out here?"

The child turned with a smile so radiant it took Annie Mac a minute to register that she had Down Syndrome. "Hey there. Would you like to come inside to see better?" Annie Mac asked. "It's warm in there."

"Twee." And the child pointed inside.

"Do you want to go see it?"

The girl nodded vehemently. "Luce?"

Annie Mac looked over at Clay. He shrugged.

"Luce come."

"Who is Luce, honey?" Annie Mac asked.

"Mine." She patted her chest. Her poor hands must be frozen.

Clay squatted on his haunches. "Is your mama near? Are you lost?"

"Mama cold. Luce come." Her enunciation was slightly off.

Clay touched Annie Mac's arm. "I wonder if Luce is her name for Louis, and she's one of the two missing children. One had Down Syndrome." He directed his question to the girl. "Honey, is your name Linney?"

She smiled and thumped her chest. "I Linney."

"And Luce is your brother Louis?"

"Luce!"

"We need to get this child inside," Annie Mac said. "She has to be freezing."

"Okay," Clay said. "I'm going to my truck to get a flashlight. I'll follow her tracks in the snow. See if I can find where she came from. And where her brother might be."

"That's good." Annie Mac took the child's cold hand. "Honey, let's go in."

She started to go with Annie Mac and then stopped. "Luce. Luce come."

"Mr. Clay is going to find your brother. You can come inside and wait with me, okay? I'm getting cold, and I bet you are, too."

Linney tilted her head to one side. Then, clinging to Annie Mac's hand, she put one foot in front of the other as they walked into the sanctuary. Voices were raised in singing "What Child Is This."

Annie Mac tried to nudge the girl to the seats next to Rita, but Linney tugged her awkwardly down the center aisle, all the way to the front. Only then did Linney stop.

She dropped Annie Mac's hand and reached up toward the tree. As the music soared from one song to another, the child's words were lost to all but those nearest her. "Twee. Linney's twee." And then she began to sing a few words, a little off key and slightly after the congregation.

Annie Mac had no idea what to do next.

Katie wasn't hampered by any of her mother's concerns. She pushed past the other children and between the shepherds to march right up to Linney. Reaching out to take the taller girl's free hand, she beamed. And then she sang the words she'd learned, "Joy to the World."

As the song ended, Katie spoke into the hush of the church, loudly enough to be heard all the way to the back. "I'm an angel. I'm supposed to take care of you."

Annie Mac looked from her girl to Linney and then up to the big cross hanging over the altar, and her eyes filled. She did nothing to stop their flow.

21 CLAY

Clay had no idea what he'd find or where the girl's footprints would take him. Snow had begun obscuring her trail, but his light picked out enough that he knew she'd come from the woods. If she'd gotten lost in there, it might take a while to find her brother because the woods wouldn't have very many footprints visible to a flashlight, not where the trees had caught the snow and kept it from the ground.

Something flickered in the darkness and then disappeared. Clay stopped, waiting for it to reappear. And then it did. A light, another flashlight.

He kept his own shining in that direction. The other light moved erratically as it came closer. Someone was running. Calling now, something unintelligible, but the voice sounded young, frantic.

Clay's light caught the figure of a boy lunging out of the woods, shielding his eyes, crying breathlessly, "Lin . . . ney, what . . . have you done with Linney?"

Clay approached the wheezing boy. "I assume you're Louis?"

The boy bent forward, gasping still. "Do you have Linney? Please don't hurt her."

"She's in the church. No one's going to hurt her. She's safe."

Louis looked ready to collapse. Clay reached out to steady him.

"I came back. She'd gone. And I saw footprints. A man's."

"Calm down. She's fine. Your sister's inside, and it's a whole lot warmer there than out here."

The boy shook his head. "Some man's in the woods. He took her. He might come after her. I looked and looked and lost their tracks."

"But she got away. That means she's safe. And she doesn't look as if anyone hurt her."

"He could come back." Louis was standing now. Steadier. But obviously still frightened.

"I'll put in a call to the sheriff's department as soon as we go in. And here's the thing," Clay said, hoping his words would calm the boy. "There are a lot of people inside that church, including me, so that's a lot of people to protect you and your sister."

Louis looked from the church back to the woods and then up to Clay. "I'd like to see her."

"Come on then."

Once they entered the sanctuary, Clay stopped behind the boy who hesitated. Must have spotted Annie Mac and Linney on the floor near the tree. And wasn't that Katie in the angel costume on Linney's other side?

Clay nudged the boy into two seats next to Rita. She smiled over at him. The congregation then stood, obscuring Linney from view.

"I'll be right back," Clay whispered and held up his phone.

Back in the narthex, he placed the call to the sheriff's office. The nearest deputy was fifteen minutes out. They'd alert State Patrol.

"I'm inside the church. The suspect is possibly in the woods back of here. Tell whoever responds to pull into the area near the storage barn, not in the church's lot. We don't need folk in a panic as service ends. I'll await word." He paused, listening to the dispatcher. "Also, please get word to Sheriff Bright. Ask him to give me a call."

"Yes, sir."

Clay slid in next to Louis and smiled down at the boy, hoping to reassure him. "Help's on the way."

"Thank you, sir."

He'd wait to talk to the sheriff before he mentioned finding the missing children. It was Christmas Eve. Rita would fix things to make sure they stayed safe.

The recessional began with "Silent Night." As people filed out, Clay spoke to Louis. "While we wait for the way to clear, I think we need to talk."

Rita, sitting next to Louis, turned toward them, but she remained silent.

Louis shook his head. "We need to find the bad man. And I need to know Linney's okay."

"I saw her when she came in and went to see the tree." Rita held out her hand. "She's fine. And my name's Rita Levinson. My job is to help women and children."

"You're not a social worker, are you?" Louis shifted away from her. He didn't shake her hand.

She dropped it and smiled. "No, I'm a lawyer."

"Oh."

"Rita," Clay said, "this is Louis. His sister's name is Linney. We need to reassure Louis that they're both safe."

"Completely safe. There's no safer place to be than in this church."

Clay's phone pinged with a text. He read it. "I need to speak to the deputy outside. Do you want to come with me?"

"N-no sir." He bit his lip, but he couldn't hide his sudden panic. "Please. You tell them?"

"I will. You stay here with Miss Rita, and I'll be right back."

Rita nodded. "We'll be fine."

"And as soon as the crowd thins, she'll take you to see your sister."

The boy's squint turned Clay's way. The kid would be seriously cute if he weren't so skinny and scared. "You're just going to turn us over to the social services people. I know. And then they'll take Linney away from me and put her in an institution or something. And they'll put me in a home with bullies who'll try to kill me." Louis crossed his arms and glared.

Clay coughed to hide a totally inappropriate grin. "I take it you've had some experience with the system."

Louis didn't respond.

"As Miss Rita said, she's a lawyer and works with kids and their mamas. So why don't we trust her to see you're safe?"

"I won't let you be hauled off tonight." Rita said. "Trust me."

Louis didn't look like he trusted anyone, but he didn't say anything else.

"The deputy may need to talk to your sister. You think you could find out something more from her?"

"She'll talk to me. But I gotta protect her. She won't talk to a policeman."

Clay didn't have jurisdiction as he'd had when Hannah wanted to keep Ty and Katie out of the system. But Sheriff Bright was a reasonable man, a family man. Surely, he'd have compassion.

Deputy Harris waited for him just outside. Clay followed him back to where two state cars and the deputy's had parked in front of the barn.

"Here's what I know so far," Clay said and began to explain the situation.

22 ANNIE MAC

As the main aisle cleared, Rita ushered a young boy forward and up to Annie Mac and her charges. Hannah and crew followed close on their heels.

"This is Louis," Rita said. "Clay's outside meeting with a deputy."

"Linney?" the boy said.

"My twee." Linney threw her arms around her brother. "My birfday twee!" Although the words came out oddly, Annie Mac understood their gist

Louis extricated himself from his sister's embrace. "She wanted a tree. That's all Linney wanted for her birthday, and I couldn't get her one."

Annie Mac nodded. "But you did get your sister a doll, didn't you?"

Louis bent his head. "Yes, ma'am, I did. I'm real sorry about that. I'll pay for the damage when I can get some money."

"Good," Annie Mac said. The boy had spunk and character.

Rita spoke up. "Clay wants Louis to ask his sister exactly what happened. I think so he can tell the deputy. Clay and I also assured Louis we'll all protect the two of them."

"I'm scared someone will send Linney to foster care. Or someplace worse." Louis crossed his arms again. "The last people hurt her because she has accidents. She can't help it."

"Oh, you poor dears." Hannah pressed forward in full rescuer mode. "We won't let that happen to you. We just *won't*."

Rita bent down to Louis's eye level and rested a hand on his shoulder. "I told you I help mothers and children in trouble, Louis. Does your mama need help?"

"We don't have a mama anymore."

Linney touched Annie Mac's cheek. "You warm. Nice. Mama wath cold."

Annie Mac explained. "Clay told us Louis and Linney lost their mama recently. Isn't that right, Louis?"

The boy bit his lower lip. Finally, eventually, he nodded.

"Do you have any other relatives?" Rita asked.

Louis shook his head, but he looked up as Father John approached. Now out of his vestments and in slacks and shirt, John said, "Clay brought me up to speed on what he's doing, but you, young man, where've you and your sister been staying?"

"We've been using your barn, sir."

The priest smiled and rested his hand on Louis's head. "I'm so glad you found a safe place. I'm Father John Ames. What's your name, son?"

"Louis Lathrop. That's my sister, Linney."

"I'm very pleased to meet you. Did you know that it's the church's job to help the homeless and take care of orphans?"

"No, sir."

"I take it you and your sister are both homeless and orphaned?"

"Mama died. Yes, sir."

"Then you've come to the right place."

"I'm real sorry I broke into your office, sir. I needed a few things, and I couldn't go far to get them, not and take care of Linney because she'd had a bad day and was very scared. And she'd lost her dolly. She was crying every night because her lion wasn't good enough. And when she wet both blankets and I knew the bathroom out in the field wasn't big enough to wash them, I had to find something to take their place. So we could stay warm."

"Of course you did."

The boy slid his glasses back up his nose, and the words tumbled out. He seemed relieved to be telling it. "But I don't know who came after Linney tonight when I went back to the store. I had to go. I made sure she was asleep before I went so she wouldn't get scared again, but the flashlight was about out of batteries, and we needed more diapers and some food. I've been trying to take real good care of her, but I was about out of ideas. We couldn't stay there forever." He paused but only for a moment. "I prayed God would send a miracle. On account of tomorrow being Linney's birthday. And it's Christmas. Even if Mama didn't believe in miracles, I kinda thought we needed one and maybe God would listen. On account of the day."

Father John sat on one of the steps leading to the altar and pulled Louis onto his ample lap. "I think, Louis, you may be the bravest boy I've ever met."

Annie Mac wasn't the only one swiping at tears. Hannah sniffled as she pulled her husband aside.

Linney stared again at the tree, Katie by her side. Annie Mac drew Ty close. Her son had been silently watching. "Take your sister to get changed, will you please."

"Now?" Ty spoke quietly.

"Please. I need to stay here with Louis and Linney, and I need you two ready to go when we've finished. Please?"

Ty didn't look happy, but he said, "Come on, Katie."

When Katie balked, Annie Mac promised she'd be right there. "Linney, too. Now you go on. Let your brother help you."

And then Clay was there, his nose red from the cold. "There's a team getting ready to search the woods, and it would help if they had more information. Louis, do you think you could get your sister to give you any details about the person who abducted her? It would help to know where he was when she got away—and how she escaped him."

Louis climbed off Father John's lap and pulled his sister away from the group. As Louis spoke, tears welled in Linney's eyes and spilled to her cheeks. She nodded. Pointed toward the woods. And then threw her arms around her brother again.

When she let go, he held her hand and brought her back into the circle. "Sometimes she's hard to understand. But I'm pretty sure she said a big man took her out of the barn and pulled her with him. She said she went until he fell and hit something and let go of her. She ran toward the lights. She could only say he was big."

"If that's all she can say, then we'll work with it," Clay said. "Thank you, Louis."

Hannah came forward, looking first at Father John, then around at the rest of them. "We'll take the children home with us tonight. And after Christmas, you, Clay, or you, Rita," she said, pointing to emphasize the words, "can figure out how to get us approved to foster them for a while. Until we see how it works."

"Foster?" Louis looked worried at her use of the word.

Annie Mac explained. "She just means she'll help out for a little while to give you a place to stay. My two children—you saw them, Ty and Katie, the little girl who was holding your sister's hand? They lived with Miss Hannah and Mr. Matt while I was in the hospital last year. They loved staying there and playing with their dog."

Hannah bent to speak directly to Louis. "We have a big house, and we have Harvey. Do you like dogs?"

"I've never had one. I don't really know."

"What about your sister? Is she afraid of animals?"

"Oh, no, she likes everything that breathes."

"We also have a big Christmas tree."

"I spoke to Sheriff Bright," Clay said to Louis. "He's going to hold off getting Social Services involved because I told him we'd take care of you two for the holidays."

"I think Hannah has the perfect solution for the holidays," Rita said. "After New Year's, we'll talk again."

"Father John?" Matt asked. "Do you have anything to add? Or to suggest?"

"No. I think you all have come up with the perfect solution. I'll pray that God will continue to lead you to know his purposes and plans."

"Then, Martin, would you mind chatting with me for a few minutes?" Matt said to Rita's husband. "I'd like to pick your brain about medical matters. It's always a plus to have all the bases covered."

Martin, a pediatrician, grinned. "I wondered if I'd be needed."

"When you two have finished," Clay said to the two men, "why don't we head out to the barn and let Louis show us what he needs from there?"

"Louis? Would you like to go home with Miss Hannah and Mr. Matt for Christmas?"

Biting his lip, Louis looked over at his sister. Tears filled his eyes, and he nodded. "Christmas."

23 Annie Mac

The phone call came just after nine Christmas morning. The Morgans were inviting everyone to help make the day festive for Louis and Linney.

"We'll be there with bells on our toes!" Annie Mac said. Then she turned to her two. "Okay, kids, let's take a look through our things and see if we can come up with something special to wrap for the two children Miss Hannah took to her house last night. They've invited us to come help them celebrate. I have the cakes I've made for everyone, but what about you two?"

They dashed into their rooms and started rummaging. Annie Mac followed Katie and watched from the doorway as her sweet girl talked to Agatha about toys to give away. It had to be hard when you were five to let go of any special item. Annie Mac looked around. "What about one of your books? You have a lot, and maybe Linney would like one of them. It would have to be one with lots of pictures."

Katie beamed up at her and wandered to her bookcase. She pulled out one, then put it back. Another out and in, then another. Finally, she came across a pop-up book of *The Night Before Christmas.* It was a little worse for wear, but Annie Mac couldn't have picked a better one herself.

"Linney likes trees. There's one here." Katie turned to the page where the tree folded out and open.

"I think she'll love it. Let's go wrap it up, okay?"

Katie carried it to Annie Mac's bedroom, where the paper and ribbons were stored. As Annie Mac finished wrapping the book, Ty wandered in. "Louis is real smart. He's a grade ahead of me, but he's only ten. So I thought he might like to play chess." Ty extended a box that contained more than just a chess set. It also had checkers, and she didn't know what else.

"Maybe you two could play together. What do you think?"

"I'm not very good at chess yet. But I can play checkers."

"There you go. I bet he'll really like that." She handed him a roll of brightly decorated wrapping paper. "Can you handle it?"

"Sure."

While he was cutting enough paper to wrap three boxes instead of one, Annie Mac opened her bureau drawer. She remembered a lilac colored sweater that was incredibly soft but unworn. She thought Auntie Sim had given it to her, but somehow lilac hadn't felt like her color. But the child's? Yes, it would be perfect and probably not too large if they rolled the sleeves once. If the girl liked it, Annie Mac could take it in and hem the sleeves.

She helped Ty fit the game box into one part of the wrapping paper and used the rest to enclose the sweater. After putting ribbons on each, she told her children to finish getting ready while she added a little make-up to her face.

Just in case.

In case of what?

She refused to think about the answer.

The adults were sitting around the Morgans' living room, enjoying eggnog and chatting, when Clay arrived. Matt let him in, brought him on back, and offered him something to drink. "There's punch, alcohol free."

"Thanks. Hey, all." He grinned around and then focused on Tadie, who was nursing Sammy. "That the heir hiding under that blanket?"

"It's lunchtime," Will answered. "Don't disturb him. The boy takes his mealtimes very seriously."

"Good appetite?" Clay dipped the ladle in the punch and filled a cup.

"Have you looked at him recently?" Tadie asked. "Chunk-a-munka here eats whatever he finds handy. Food, toys, milk."

They laughed. "He's a healthy one," his Auntie Hannah said. "And a charmer."

"Where are the kids?" Clay took a seat.

"Upstairs," Hannah said. "Louis is showing off his new room. Linney and Katie are playing dolls."

Clay glanced around and caught Annie Mac's eye for a moment before speaking to the room in general. "Searcher found the man who'd gone after Linney. He broke an ankle when he tripped, then tried to crawl out of the woods. He gave up and pulled pine needles over himself so he wouldn't freeze."

"I take it," Matt said, "he's incarcerated at the moment?"

"He is, but I'm not sure how long they'll be able to hold him unless Linney's capable of identifying him."

"Oh, no," Hannah said. "That could traumatize her."

"It could," Clay said. "But he ought to pay for what he almost did." He glanced up the stairs. "We should ask Louis what he thinks she can handle."

"Those poor children." Tadie shifted Samuel. The baby sat up and gave everyone a satisfied smile.

Annie Mac smiled back. What a cutie. Sammy would never feel the sort of desperation Louis had—and maybe still did. Or the fear hers had known.

"How's it going with Linney?" Clay asked Hannah.

"She's so precious. She wanted Louis to sleep in her bed, but I read to her and then sang to her until she drifted off. She woke once during the night, but that was good, as I was able to get her to the toilet before she wet the diaper." Hannah brushed at a tear. "I don't know how that dear boy managed. Father John had it right. He's about the bravest boy I've ever seen." She shifted to look at Annie Mac. "Yours is, too. You know I adore Ty, but there's something about a ten-year-old boy taking such care of an older sister. It's too much. Just breaks my heart."

"You don't want to get too attached now," Clay said. "They might have other kin. You may just have to give them up."

Hannah shook her head. "I know. I've had practice with that, haven't I?"

And didn't that just tug at Annie Mac's heart?

Matt sat down next to his wife and wrapped his arm around her. But he didn't speak. They all knew Hannah'd faced losses of her own and then had fallen for Ty and Katie. She'd never been able to keep a child, had she? Annie Mac looked up the stairs and then back at Hannah.

God, are Hannah and Matt your answers for those two orphans?

If so, she sure hoped God meant it long term, for everyone's sake.

The doorbell rang again, this time bringing Agnes and Brisa into the group. How kind Hannah was, including them. Including all of the group. Hannah'd told them Rita and Martin would have been here if they hadn't been spending the day with her mama and daddy and heading off to church with them in the afternoon.

Hannah waved Brisa upstairs to join the kids and offered Agnes something to drink. Food had been set out on the dining table for anyone to take when they were hungry.

Agnes wouldn't accept Matt's place beside Hannah but chose the ottoman near Clay. Hannah asked Tadie something, and Matt and Will started chatting. Annie Mac, standing to fix a plate of snacks, overheard Agnes's words to Clay.

"I didn't know Henry's brother goes to your church."

"Eric?" Clay asked. "I conned him into going for last night's program only because he didn't have any other plans. I think he's so new to town he feels at loose ends, especially when his brother's working." He sipped his punch. "You had last night off?"

"Because of Brisa. She was thrilled to be in the pageant."

"That's one gorgeous girl you've got there, Agnes," Annie Mac said on her way back to her seat.

Agnes smiled. "Thank you." But she didn't have much else to say, Annie Mac noted, and she seemed uncomfortable, not just because of her seat on the ottoman, but among all these people.

And yet hadn't Annie Mac also felt strange with everyone in the beginning? And now look at her.

Clay continued chatting with Agnes after Annie Mac had moved too far away to hear. Eventually, with him, Agnes seemed to relax.

Annie Mac glanced away as unwanted thoughts flew through her head. Just how well did Agnes know Clay? And how did she know him?

Agnes was single, Clay was single.

Annie Mac had sent Clay on his way. Clay wanted to be a father. Brisa needed a father.

Annie Mac set her plate down and stood abruptly. "I think I'll go check on the kids."

"Good idea," Hannah said.

Clay ignored her. Of course he did. He was too engrossed in talking to Agnes.

The kids were fine. Certainly they were fine.

Ty sat across from Louis on one of the twin beds as Louis coached him in the finer points of chess. They looked so cute, one blonde, one brown haired with glasses he constantly had to push up his nose. He needed a trip to the optometrist. Hannah could manage that.

Brisa and Jilly perched on the other bed. Brisa had brought a comb, mirror, and brush set for Linney. Instead of Linney using it, the two older girls were grooming each other.

She couldn't technically call Brisa and Jilly older, though, could she? They weren't twelve yet. But twelve-year-old Linney would probably never actually be older in her mind. Which, at the moment, made her a perfect playmate for Katie.

And weren't they cute?

Annie Mac sat in the rocker to watch them. This must be the guest room, but Hannah had changed it quickly into a room for a little girl, who was actually not small. Hannah knew about bed-wetters from having Katie stay here, which meant she'd certainly taken precautions. Speaking of which . . .

"Girls," Annie Mac. "Katie, Linney, I think it's time we made a quick trip to the bathroom."

Katie bounced up. "You come, too, Linney. We have to remember to go so we don't have accidents."

Linney took a moment to process what Katie wanted and then stood, took Katie's hand, and went with her to the bathroom. Annie Mac followed in case she was needed, but Katie helped her bigger friend and then went herself.

Annie Mac found it fascinating that Katie seemed to know Linney was a special girl, without Annie Mac or anyone saying anything. Thinking how Katie'd come out of the angel choir to help, Annie Mac felt another powerful tug of love.

When Katie flushed the toilet, she reminded Linney they had to wash their hands. The two girls giggled as they compared the soapy suds on their fingers before rinsing them. By the time they'd returned to Linney's room, Annie Mac knew she wasn't needed there. She started to go downstairs when Brisa and Jilly raced past. "We're hungry," Jilly explained.

Annie Mac laughed. Until she got downstairs and found Agnes still chatting with Clay and Brisa scooting in between them, giving Clay an up-close-and-very-personal look at the beauty of that young girl who didn't have a daddy. Clay was a sucker for needy kids, wasn't he? And Brisa was looking at him as if she wanted nothing more than to climb in *his* lap.

Annie Mac wanted to call her two down and tell them to block the new girl's moves.

And then she heard her own thoughts and headed immediately for the downstairs powder room. After locking the door, she stared at her miserable self.

"You, my girl, deserve your nightmares and your lonely life. Nasty, jealous, miserable cow, that's what you are."

She closed her eyes, made a fist, and pressed it to her stomach, trying to keep the bile down there instead of having it seep up to her throat. Maybe Hannah would let the kids stay for a little while, and she could get away. Get home or go for a walk now that the snow had mostly melted.

Taking a deep breath, she flushed the toilet so no one would think she'd come in here only to rant at herself and casually approached Hannah. She spoke softly for Hannah's ears only. "I'm not feeling well. Would you mind if the kids stayed here for an hour or two so I can go home, maybe take a nap?"

"Oh, honey, not at all. You just take yourself on home. We'll be fine. And don't you worry about coming back for them. We'll keep them long as you need a break. You've been so busy all week, working on that pageant. No wonder you're feeling exhausted."

Annie Mac excused herself to the group, collected her coat, and left Hannah to explain her absence to the children. "They'll be fine, Annie Mac. It'll be especially good for Louis and Linney. Think of this as you doing me a favor."

They hugged, and Annie Mac headed back outside and down the drive. In the crisp air, she felt slightly foolish. No, completely foolish.

But she needed to be alone so she could have a good cry and a good yell and maybe even a nap.

That was all she needed. Rest and time to let all the good and positive things in her life settle until she believed in them. Because she was now a woman on her way to total independence. She had a good job. Soon she'd have a new home. Really, life was great.

24 CLAY

Clay didn't buy that bit about Annie Mac's exhaustion. Well, he did, because she probably was exhausted and stressed with all she'd been doing and the move she'd have to make.

But the notion that only her physical state had taken her away didn't sit well with him. And what got him to say his own goodbyes a half-hour later were the looks she kept sending Agnes as he and the waitress talked. It hadn't meant anything, of course, their talk.

He'd told Agnes about Eric's boat—she'd been curious—and then she'd asked, in a roundabout way, about Henry's. He couldn't be much help there, except to say he'd seen it from a distance, and it looked like Henry was working hard to get it in shape.

Then they'd talked about sailing—of which she knew nothing—and about twins—again, nothing, but he didn't have a clue either. She'd wondered—again, offhandedly—if Eric was in Beaufort as a watchdog for his brother. But Clay wouldn't comment on something that was only Eric's business.

When Brisa came down and cuddled with her mama, close enough for him to be uncomfortable—and wasn't that child going to be a handful very soon—he caught a sick look on Annie Mac's face as she glanced from Brisa up to where her children played.

Annie Mac's look *had* meant something. He'd bet on it. *What* it had meant was something he intended to find out.

"Hannah, Matt, thanks so much for inviting me. I'm gonna head out now. Tell Louis I'll be back to talk to him in the morning."

Goodbyes said, he showed himself out and got in his car. It was only three blocks to Annie Mac's, but he didn't want his Jeep where anyone would see it. He found a place to park on a side street, walked around the corner and up the stairs. Then he knocked on her door.

She didn't answer. He knocked again. She finally opened it a crack. And then all the way.

"I wanted to check on you." He stuffed his fingers in his front pockets.

She didn't smile. "I'm fine."

"I suppose that's why you look like you've been crying since you left."

She grabbed a tissue out of her pocket and swiped it under her eyes. It had black smudges when she finished. "Great. I forgot I wore mascara today."

He grinned. "I've seen you in all your glory, Annie Mac. You don't have to be embarrassed in front of me."

Her shoulders slumped. "I was trying to be beautiful."

He tilted up her chin. "Annie Mac, you are beautiful. Always."

"Hah."

He turned her toward the living room and pushed her down on the couch and then sat beside her. "That, my good woman, is the crux of the matter. You don't believe anything I say or do."

"What do you mean? I do believe you."

He took her hand and held it lightly in his. "No, you don't. If you did, you'd believe me when I tell you you're beautiful."

"But that would be—"

"And you don't believe me when I tell you I love you. I don't think you even know what love is."

She snatched her hand back. "I do. I love my kids."

He sighed. "Okay. You love your kids. So, when Ty misbehaves or Katie talks back, do you decide you no longer love them?"

She glared at him. "Of course not."

"What about when they're sick?"

"You're being ridiculous."

"What if one of them had been born with Down Syndrome? Or some other handicap?"

"What are you getting at, Clay? This conversation seems to be moving from ridiculous to absurd."

He was afraid of the next part. Would he be betraying Ty if he brought it up? Or had Ty told him so he'd try to fix things?

"Should someone not love you because you have nightmares?"

That got her attention. She scooted away, fluttered her hands at him, and stood abruptly. "How? How do you know about those? No one knows."

"Ty does. He's worried about you." He leaned back and draped his arms on the back of the couch. She looked so cute, furious like that.

"Oh, great." The word came out on a puff of mad. "Now my own son thinks I'm crazy. What, did he come to you, suggesting you fix me? You, Mr. Fix-Everything police lieutenant, who's made my kids fall in love with you so they keep pushing me to get on board."

Clay sent up a quick prayer. He should have prayed before knocking on her door, but maybe God could work retroactively. *Help me out here, please?*

He should have prepared what he'd say, too. Figured it all out. But it was too late now. He stood.

She gave him her back. It was a lovely back, with lovely long red hair, and his fingers itched to stroke it.

He tucked the tips of those fingers back into his pockets, away from temptation. "It's not like that."

"No?" She turned to face him. "No? Then what's it like? The crazy woman who can't sleep through the night without screaming? You'd like to marry that woman?" Her voice rose, whether in fury or panic, he wasn't sure. "You'd like to share a bed with someone who might haul off and flail so hard that she smashes a fist into your nose *because she thinks you're him?* The man who tried to kill her? Is that what you want?"

He stood taller, anger shoring him up. "Have you ever thought about it from my perspective? Have you ever, in all your worries and fears, considered that maybe you wouldn't want to be married to a man who has some scars, who sometimes has to get up in the middle of the night because he's needed? A man who just might reach over in the middle of your nightmare and pull you close and hug you and *make you feel safe?*"

Her eyes grew wide.

"No," he said, warming to his fury. "You're too self-absorbed to think what your rejection does to me. You're too blind to anyone else's needs, too sure you're right, to understand that love means more than finding someone perfect, and only someone perfect, to whom you give your heart. That love means caring for the loved one if he's wounded, if she's broken, if he's imperfect, if he makes mistakes, if she gets fat or wrinkly or forgetful. It means putting someone else first, and, Annie Mac, you're lying to yourself if you think by keeping me at arm's length you've been protecting me and putting me first. That's not love. That's fear."

She still didn't speak. But she didn't move either.

Raking his fingers through his hair, he took a deep breath as he tried to rein in his emotions. Ranting at her wouldn't produce anything but higher blood pressure. He softened his tone. "What does the Bible say about love and fear? It claims that 'Perfect love casts out all fear.'"

This time, her tears spilled one after the other. When she didn't dry them, he did. His thumb wiped off first one and then another. "Annie Mac, I love you."

She shook her head, sighing.

He repeated the words. "I love you." And then one more time. "I love you. I don't love a perfect woman. I don't love a woman without issues. I don't *want* a woman like that."

He waited for her to respond, but she backed further away and dropped her chin. "I *can't.* I just can't." She crossed her arms over her chest as if to protect herself.

From him. He stilled, taking that in. He'd poured out his heart, and she'd handed it back, unwanted.

Cold washed over him as if he'd fallen between numbing ice flows with no way out. But he didn't panic. He accepted his fate. Finally.

"I'm sorry. I shouldn't have come." And he turned and walked to the door. Before opening it, he looked once more over his shoulder. "I won't bother you again. Take care, Annie Mac. I wish you a happy life."

And then he strode out into the cold daylight.

25 ANNIE MAC

She watched the door close. His heart close.

Her heart shatter.

Her world shatter.

She'd said no. Again.

What had his words been? The whisper of them came to her. "I don't love a perfect woman. I don't love a woman without issues. I don't *want* a woman like that."

He'd spoken them so gently. So softly.

"Perfect love casts out fear."

The memory of those words flailed her as she stood, broken, longing.

For what could never be.

God? O God, please. Please.

He was gone. She'd pushed him away for the very last time.

His footsteps receded down the stairs. Away. He'd be in his car in a minute. And gone.

And *she*—no one else—*she* had done it. She'd sent him away.

What had she done?

Suddenly, she wanted to take her refusal back. All of it . . . back.

She rushed to the door and flung it open. He stood at his Jeep, his hands braced on the car roof, his head bowed. He must have heard her, because he slowly looked up.

She covered her lips with her fingers. Tears cascaded down. Her shoulders shook.

He merely stared. She'd hurt him too much, hadn't she? Shattered his hopes one too many times.

She extended a hand in supplication. "Please?"

He waited.

"Will you come back inside?"

He didn't move. She stood, waiting, too. Letting the cold air from outside mingle with the warmer air escaping through her open door. Praying. Begging with her eyes.

"Please?"

He pushed away from the car. Nodded once and came toward her. She didn't move. When he'd reached the top of the stairs, she ushered him inside, then closed the door behind them.

"I'm sorry," she said.

His eyes were cold, shuttered. "Did you ask me to come all the way up here just so you could say you're sorry?" His voice was as cold as his eyes.

She had hurt him beyond redemption. When he'd been most vulnerable, most open, she'd rejected him. "I was wrong." She wanted to reach for him, but he looked too big, too unwelcoming.

"About what?" His eyes had narrowed, but she felt something shift in him. A miniscule crack in his armor.

"I'm scared," she said, her voice low, afraid. She was afraid on so many levels. Afraid she'd hurt him too much to fix this. Afraid of how much she needed him. Wanted him.

"And you think I'm not?" he said. "You think I haven't wanted to get over loving you, move on with my life, find someone I didn't have to convince to *want me*? You think I like having my love, my very *self,* tossed back in my face again and again?"

"I thought I wanted you to move on, even if I couldn't move past you myself. Even if I couldn't shut down my feelings."

"And now?" He stepped closer, tipped her chin up. "Tell me the truth, Annie Mac. The truth from your heart."

"The truth is, I don't deserve you. I don't deserve what you're offering. And I'm a broken mess of a woman."

"Oh, Annie Mac." He shook his head. His voice had softened enough to give her—what? Hope? "Don't you realize I'm also imperfect and broken, that I have issues of my own?"

She straightened, backed until she could look into his eyes without having to tilt her head so much. "I think you want to rescue us, like you did last year. I don't want to be rescued. And I don't want anyone else having to deal with my craziness."

"Whoa." And then he seemed to think about her words. "Okay. Maybe it's partly true, the rescue bit. But did you ever think that I might need rescuing just as much? That I might need you as much as you need me?"

She waited, because the idea of Clay needing to be rescued seemed absurd.

"Sometimes, it's just that way," he said. "God gives us people to love who meet our craziness with some of their own, who fit our neediness with their wholeness and let us fit our whole places to their needy ones. He doesn't fix us without a little pain, and he lets us have both the pain and the imperfections because other people need us that way." He reached out and clasped both her hands. She let him. "And we need them that way."

"Do we?" Could he possibly need her messes? She didn't know how. "Why?"

"Think about it. If we were never challenged to deal with another person's imperfections, we wouldn't change and grow, would we?"

"I guess not." But it sounded uncomfortable, especially because she'd be the truly messed-up one in their pairing. "Still, it seems more logical—more *rational*—for people to try to get fixed first. Maybe that would cut down on the divorce rate." It would probably also mean she'd be alone forever, because fixing herself didn't seem to be happening. She felt cold creeping over her and hugged herself again.

He shook his head. "Based on my experience—"

"You have a lot?" That came out badly. "Sorry."

He raised that mobile brow of his. "Let me finish. I'm talking about basic interpersonal relationships now. God seems to put us together with people—at work, in families, in friendships—to help us grow. Sort of like stones in the water, rubbing against each other as the water flows over them until they're each smooth. If each stone sat alone, not touching anything and out of the stream of that water, it wouldn't ever smooth out, would it?"

"Probably not." Now they were supposed to knock together like stones?

"So, how about you risk rubbing together with me so we can both smooth out?"

"That, sir, sounds painful."

He sighed and then turned it into a grin. "I'm trying to make the offer sound reasonable to you, and you go all literal on me. What am I going to do with you, Annie Mac?"

"Talk flowers instead of rocks?"

"Which flowers do you like best?"

"I don't know. I love them all, but maybe daffodils. They look so hopeful."

"We'll plant a field of daffodils. Does that work?"

Her eyes filled. He seemed so eager to please, but all she had to offer was a nod and a whisper. "I love daffodils in the spring."

He pulled her close until she had to drop her arms to her sides. She felt his breath on her forehead. She stared at his shirt collar, there where his neck met it, the tanned skin close to her, smelling of clean male and the soap he used. It brought memories flooding in of being in his home, of the scents that filled it, always fresh and clean. A yearning welled in her to return to that place with its view of the creek, with its comforts. A safe place where this man had made them welcome, and she'd first fallen in love.

"Annie Mac," he whispered, his voice husky. "I need you to let me shower you with daffodils."

She didn't answer. He took her chin again. Lifted it and stared into her eyes. His gaze lowered to her lips.

He was waiting for her to say something, to do something, wasn't he? She let her own gaze touch his lips. Her breathing accelerated. Her lips parted, but she didn't speak.

And he lowered his head until his lips touched hers, softly, briefly. She heard a moan. It had to have come from her. He pressed the kiss and took her lips thoroughly, deeply, wrapping his arms around her, lifting her to his height, drawing her as close as she fit.

She circled his neck with her arms as he deepened the kiss even more. She returned it with all the pent-up fervor she could manage. This was it, finally, the thing she'd longed for, the lips she'd coveted for far, far too long.

After he lowered her to stand toe to toe with him, she put aside the momentary panic she felt from being released, from trying to stand on her own, to breathe more evenly, to think.

"Annie Mac," he finally whispered on a breath.

She stepped back, still unsteady, bracing herself on his forearms. "I've never . . ."

"I know. I haven't either."

His words brought her out of her daze. What did he mean? "You haven't what?"

He grinned. "Kissed and been kissed just like that. You take away my breath."

"Oh. Yeah. That's what I was trying to say."

"Time to fess up, Annie Mac. I need to hear the words."

Here it went. He wanted stone against stone. Panic tried to sneak back in. She took another step back. "You know the words." Heat rose up her neck, to her cheeks.

"Annie Mac . . . "

She bit her lip.

"The words? I said them three times." At least he smiled.

"You did, didn't you?" Her blush remained, but she twinkled up at him. Who knew she could flirt? "You really want them?"

"I need them."

"Ooh. Need, eh?"

"Need. See, I'm secure enough in my manhood—"

"You ought to be."

"I'm secure enough that I can admit a need for your words."

She'd needed his, hadn't she? She closed the gap between them, pulled his head down, and whispered in his ear. "I love you, too."

He straightened. "Annie Mac." He said her name reproachfully. "That's the best you can do? Because I want the woman I marry to be able to say it any time and all the time."

"Marry? Your last proposal was more flowery than that."

"Well, look how well that one worked out." He sounded grouchy. "I figured this time I'd just stake my claim and be done with it."

She giggled—and the strangeness of the sound surprised her. She thought it might have been her first giggle since girlhood. "Clay Dougherty, I love you. I really do. But I'm warning you, I'm a lot to handle.

And if you end up with a broken nose one night because you didn't react quickly enough, you can't say I didn't warn you."

"We'll sleep with a pillow between us. You can beat it up instead of me. I have a very big bed."

"I like to snuggle."

"You do?"

She considered that, trying to remember if she'd ever snuggled with anyone other than her children. "Well, I *think* I do. I think I might."

"First black eye, and a pillow goes between us."

"Deal."

She remembered what she hadn't told him. "You may not know that you'll be marrying a newly permanent member of the teaching staff at Beaufort Elementary."

"Ah, a woman of means." He kissed the tip of her nose. "A two income family. Next you'll be insisting on vacations in Europe."

"Paris!" The possibilities seemed endless. "I'm feeling dizzy. A few days ago I was on the verge of homelessness and poverty. Then I shifted income brackets with one phone call. And now I'm contemplating marriage and a family trip to France."

"I was thinking honeymoon first."

She arched her brows. "You think that's going to work?"

"We're going to have a terrible time keeping either of them down on the farm," he said mournfully, but the twinkle was there. "Can you picture what Katie will do to the men of Paris? And Ty? He'll want to climb the Eiffel Tower."

A few kisses later, she asked, "Do you want to go back to the Morgans'? To tell the kids." She heard a wistful note in her own voice.

"Do you?"

"Only if you do."

"I don't. I want to stay right here and kiss you senseless and then tell the kids that fairly soon—I'm thinking as soon as Father John will do the honors—they'll be able to call me dad. What do you think?"

The thought of that almost had her knees buckling, but she stiffened them and kissed his chin. "I'd like that." And then she grinned. "You do know I'll be marrying you for your house."

"Ho-ho. I'd forgotten your landlord's ultimatum. That's fine. You can marry me for my house, but I'm marrying you for your kids."

"Stinker."

"What can I say? Katie has killer eyelashes. She won my heart the first time she flashed them at me. And Ty? Well, he likes to sail. A man's gotta have a son to take sailing."

"We need to tell them."

"We will. First, I promised you some more kisses."

"Oh, right. I'd forgotten."

He reminded her then, again and again. And he promised her a lot more. Very soon.

25 Louis

Louis slid one hand over the big-boy blazer and the pants Miss Hannah had bought for him. She'd found him a bow tie, too, one that almost matched Mr. Matt's. They were sitting one row back from the front, him and Linney and Mr. Matt and Miss Hannah. Linney looked so pretty in the blue dress Miss Hannah had gotten her to go with her eyes, and she wore a big blue bow in her hair. Linney's hair was always clean now, and she was so much better about using the potty.

All she'd needed was a happy place. What a difference happy made. For him, too. Now, he could breathe.

He sat up a little straighter. God sure had fixed it so they got found by good people. Found and fixed. Linney had her new glasses, pretty ones with light blue rims. And she was having her ears looked at. And his own glasses didn't slip down anymore.

Miss Hannah'd been tutoring him so he'd be ready for school when it started up again. She and Mr. Matt had so many books. Books about *everything.*

They had friends, him and Linney. Katie'd come to play with Linney lots, and Ty and he were pretty much best friends now. Ty didn't mind him being brainy. As a matter of fact, Ty said it was really cool to have a smart friend. Ty wasn't stupid, and he'd turned into a decent chess player. It was really cool the way they could talk about all kinds of things.

Miss Rita and her husband sat a few seats down from them, in the same row. Miss Rita had gone hunting and made sure Mama didn't have any other relatives alive, at least none who claimed them, and she'd gotten approval for them to stay with Miss Hannah. The way Miss Hannah and Mr. Matt talked about it, they wanted him and Linney to be their very own kids.

They'd said that's what they were going to ask the courts, and what did he and Linney think about it?

He'd gotten so choked up, he hadn't known what to do. Linney'd looked at him because she didn't understand, but with his throat full like that, he couldn't tell her. Not without everybody knowing.

Miss Hannah had patted her lap, and Linney'd gone to her, climbing on like the little girl she wasn't. "Sweet girl, do you know what a mommy is?"

Linney'd nodded her head. "Mama gone."

"Yes, your mama is gone. Would you like to have a new mommy?"

Linney's hands had reached up, one on each of Miss Hannah's cheeks, and she'd said, "Mommy?"

Just like that. Louis's tears had really spilled then, and Mr. Matt had pulled him close and whispered in his ear and said the word "son." All Louis could do was nod his head against Mr. Matt's shoulder and imagine calling him "dad."

A dad of his own. A real dad and a mother who didn't make him do all the clean-up and taking care of?

The wonder of Linney was that she could love without thinking much. If you were good to her, she'd give you the moon back. That was exactly what happened. Miss Hannah looked like Linney'd gone and done that, given her the moon. She pulled Louis's sister into her arms and squeezed and squeezed, and Linney squeezed right back.

Not more than a minute later, Linney cried out, "Mommy!" before she turned and shouted the word to him. "Mommy!" And then she squeezed Miss Hannah again.

Mr. Matt watched, and then he turned back to Louis. Maybe he needed something more. Anyway, Mr.

Matt looked all serious now with his eyes dried. "What about you? I've never been a dad, but I'd really like to give it a shot."

And Louis, who still couldn't speak, nodded and rubbed at his eyes and prayed they'd never change their minds, because he wanted to give being Mr. Matt's kid a shot, too.

Now here they were. It was twilight again. Back when she was well, Mama used to say twilight was the best part of the day and had taken some poets words. He'd called it "the silent hour." They used to sit on the front stoop, watching as the stars started blinking on, and everything seemed perfect.

Hadn't it been twilight when Linney first saw the church tree? The one that had called her here? It had certainly been a twilight Christmas, God pouring gifts on them.

The big inside tree blinked at him now with its hundreds of lights. And candles were lit at the altar again, as they had been that night. Even if it was getting dark outside, in here, everything was light. And it smelled like Christmas ought to, even if they were already in January. Louis was real glad they'd left the tree and the decorations up for tonight, because tonight Mr. Clay and Miss Annie Mac and Louis's best friend Ty and Linney's best friend Katie would walk up that aisle to claim their own miracle.

Ty'd told him how patient Mr. Clay had been, waiting on his mom to get with the program to marry

Mr. Clay. He and Katie'd wanted nothing more than to have the man he called the lieutenant be their very own dad.

It looked to Louis like God had really been busy this Christmas making good things happen all around. Yep, God seemed big enough for just about anything.

Anything at all.

THE END

ACKNOWLEDGEMENTS

This short book came out of a thought that blossomed into thousands of words flying off my fingertips and into the computer faster than I've ever seen in all my years of writing. That *never* happens to this writing slogger. But first drafts always need fixing. Even second and third drafts do. I am so grateful to Jennifer Fromke and Robin Patchen for their slashing and chopping and egging me on to make it better, to dig a little deeper. And after the digging and the rewriting, they put on their editor hats and worked magic. Their thoughtful suggestions were invaluable.

A few members of my Street Team did the eagle-eye proofing again. I am so grateful to DJ Sakata, Susan Peterson, Becky Hrivnak, and Carol Boyer. I don't know what I'd do without these ladies. They, along with Ariana, my brave and valiant first born, provoke me to offer my best, my very best.

A special thank you goes out to all those encouragers who have blessed me over the years and always and every day to my beloved husband and my mama, who give me time.

What Others Are Saying

About **_Becalmed_** **Carolina Coast Novel, Book 1**
It's a rare book that draws you in from the first page, wraps its cover around you, and warmly envelops you in its unfolding tale. This book did that for me... ~Lita Smith-Mines, _Boating Times of Long Island_

About **_Heavy Weather_** **Carolina Coast Book 2**
...the book's strengths lie in its suspense and vivid characters, whose personalities and small-town relationships are truly believable. A heavy, suspenseful North Carolina novel about parenthood, human connection, and how to make peace with the cards you're dealt. ~_Kirkus Reviews_

About **_Sailing out of Darkness_**
...beautiful, gorgeous imagery... It is take your breath away awesomeness. The storyline could absolutely suck and I wouldn't care half as much because I just wanted to read more descriptions of people, places, feelings and thoughts. This is true writing talent here. And she's a wonderful storyteller too. ~_Samantha Coville, Sammy the Bookworm_

About **_From Fire into Fire_** **An Isaac's House Novella**
...a riveting story pulled right out of current events

...an excellent novella written by an accomplished novelist.

About *Two from Isaac's House,* An Isaac's House Novel

...Fischer's novel is nothing less than thoroughly gripping! ~Top Pick, *Romantic Times* Book Reviews